Bill's Lengthy Atonement
Book II: *The Future*

Norman Merwarth

GatorTales Publishing—The Villages, Florida
ISBN: 979-8-9897064-1-9
Library of Congress Control Number: 2024924591
Title: *Bill's Lengthy Atonement: Book II: The Future*
Author: Norman Merwarth
Digital distribution | 2024
Paperback | 2024

Published in the United States by New Book Authors Publishing

Dedication

This is for my wonderful wife of 61 years, Carole. You are my best friend, my travel companion, my lover, my fine dining and drinking buddy and my biggest fan no matter what kind of crazy thing I attempt. You have always had my back, and I will love you forever!

Prologue

The year is now 2088. Could it actually be possible? Could the seemingly indestructible, very well loved and very highly respected Sunny and BD Turner have passed away? Cards, letters, emails, messages from every type of media and phone calls of condolences from all over came flooding in to their kids, Danny and Ashley, and to the 4 grandchildren, Dean, Christy, Soleada, and Ben. Sunny and BD had helped so many people over their 65 years together that many of the condolences would bring the readers to tears. There were even quite a few from other countries. They claimed that visiting The Villages in Florida and touching the statue of Chewie, Sunny's Golden Retriever miracle dog, in the town square of Eastport had cured them and allowed them to live very long lives. Danny, Ashley, their partners and their 4 kids often discussed how they all seemed to be blessed with good health, good luck and happiness, and they made it a ritual to hold hands and say a prayer to who or what was in control whenever they had a gathering. If they only knew! If they only knew!

Chapter 1
Reminiscing Down Below

Chief Danny Turner was reading some reports on the wide screen in the dashboard as he arrived at the postal center in the Village of Hawkins and let his new 2088 squad car park itself. He marveled at all of the technological advances made to the police vehicles over the many years he had been a police officer. All were now EVs with new types of light weight solid state batteries that could be charged in less than a minute and had ranges of at least 1000 miles. All had long ago achieved flawless self driving capability, were electronically protected, were bullet proof and had airless "never flat" tires. He couldn't remember the last time any of his men had gotten lost or stranded while on duty. The old criticisms about EVs catching fire, breaking down and taking forever to charge were long in the past. Almost no one attempted to flee from the cops anymore, and if they did try they were quickly apprehended. Everyone's vehicle could be easily tracked, and the latest police car models could disable a fleeing car electronically with just a push of a button. Every once in a while, however, some guy would get an old ICE vehicle out of storage and find enough very expensive gas to go zooming down the turnpike at up to 200 mph. There were some amusing videos of police chases circulating online. Rapid response police drones of all sizes holding up to 4 people were being used in many situations, but they presented whole new problems. Personal "civilian operated drones" had been tried for years with many disastrous accidents and were finally banned. Only specially licensed corporate drones and hundreds of thousands of "taxi type drones" were being used, and even those required massive computer power and programming to keep from having serious crashes. Being a cop today was very different from when his father, BD, was the Sumter County Police Chief.

Danny had decided to take the old road to this location to refresh his memory of where his dad had pretty much trashed his old 2022 squad car rushing to try to get to his mom's rescue. He passed the roundabout that his dad jumped at 100 mph, and the gouges on the low curbing on both sides were still visible after all these years. The palms, oak trees and shrubbery in the roundabout were now fully mature and would have prevented such an Evel Knievel type jump today. That old picture of the trashed squad car still hangs in the police headquarters along with pictures of Chewie and Braveheart. It is a daily routine after every shift's briefing for all officers to pass by the pictures touching them for good luck. Only once did a rookie forget to do it, and that day he was broadsided in an intersection by a red light runner. That was about 20 years ago, and no one failed to stick to the routine after that day. Danny had instructed the car to slowly pass through the old neighborhood of patio villas where he and his sister lived for several years as young kids, and he was amazed at the huge, old growth oak trees, palms, magnolias and shrubs. The vinyl sided homes looked much the same, but he could barely remember the neighborhood. An old couple waved from the entrance of the lanai at the villa he had lived in. While waving back, he wondered if they knew about the events that took place there before he was born.

It was going to be a bittersweet day for the Turner gang when they would meet up on the walking trail around the wetlands at the new memorial bench installed for his mother, Sunny, and father, BD Turner. Danny picked up a box with the two urns containing his parents ashes and headed toward the walking trail. He was warmly greeted by many walkers, as Chief Turner was extremely popular in the lowest crime area in the state of Florida. Much of it was due to the efforts of his father, old Poppop and Jorge's company with their house hardening efforts over the many years since the near catastrophic break in at his mom's villa. He thought back about the hundreds of times he and his sister Ashley begged to be told the exciting story about their mom's beautiful Golden Retriever, Chewie, losing his life while saving hers. He could picture old Poppop with his .45 swinging up and blasting 3 holes in the SOB who would have taken her life. He could also picture his dad running through the trashed house just seconds later with his 9mm service weapon at the ready. The four grandkids must have asked to hear the story of that night a thousand times, and it never got old. They had dearly loved their grandparents and couldn't believe they both died within 3 days of one another. That night was such a big deal in The Villages over 65 years ago, that some old guy even wrote a fairly accurate novel about the events. Danny had purchased a copy and read it several times. It was called *Bill's Lengthy Atonement* and was written by an 80 year old Villager, Norman "somebody." He couldn't remember the last name, but Danny still had that old novel stashed away in his office and decided to read it again when he had a chance.

Danny arrived at the new memorial bench located almost a mile from the parking area, and he loved the location they had chosen. It looked out over the wetlands and the trail where his parents had walked almost daily with Chewie and then with Braveheart. He had trouble remembering that day when Braveheart saved his sister from being kidnapped. He was only 4 years old, but he remembered a lot of commotion and having to take Braveheart to the Vet. Lost in thought, he finally looked up to catch a glimpse of Ashley's beautiful strawberry blonde hair in the distance. She looked just like their mother at that age and was also a rehab nurse with an excellent reputation. He and his sister got along famously, and he couldn't remember ever arguing with her. He could see that she was carrying a box. Mom and Dad wanted their ashes scattered together as soon as possible, but they never mentioned what to do with the ashes of Chewie and Braveheart. Ashley was bringing them to scatter along with the ashes of the two people who had loved them so much. When she arrived they both warmly hugged each other.

Ashley said, "I'm glad we are early so we can talk until the kids arrive. This location is perfect under the huge live oak trees and looking out over the wetlands. I love these plaques you had made for the bench. Mom and Dad would have loved to see that the dogs were also mentioned."

Danny and she started talking about the wonderful marriage their parents had and how they were always smiling at each other, holding hands, touching each other, hugging, kissing and never arguing.

Danny said, "Yep Sis, I remember us always talking about how we wanted to have partners like that, and I think we hit the jackpot. I think it was fate or something else urging me to stop in at Jorge's business office to see how things were going. I could literally feel something telling me to turn the car around."

"Then you saw the beautiful Maria Sunny Ortega and gave her the old 'cow eyes,'" said Ashley, laughing out loud.

Danny smiled and said, "I was dumbstruck and acting all goofy, and I felt like an idiot. Finally I just blurted out, 'Please go out with me!' She was laughing her butt off, and I was amazed when she said, 'Sure, where are we going?' Now wait a second Sis, since you were talking about the old 'cow eyes,' how about when I introduced you to my cop friend, Andy Anderson. I thought your eyeballs were going to fall out. You both turned beet red. It was a perfect match."

"He was and still is handsome. I thought he was so serious, but it turned out he was just shy. He treats me so well Danny. We were blessed for sure, and I see how you and Maria still look at each other."

Suddenly Ashley had tears running down her face, and Danny asked if she was ok.

"I was thinking about the last two months when Mom started going downhill so fast. I just can't believe that researchers can still not find a cure for ALS after all these years. When Mom asked if Dad would take her to the Sawgrass Grove area for one last dance, because that is where they had their first dance together, of course he said yes. When they showed up, Mom was in her wheelchair, and everybody recognized them and made room up front for them. Dad asked if the band could play 'Unchained Melody' by the Righteous Brothers from many years ago. It so happened that they could. Dad easily picked Mom up and carried her in his arms like a child, in a slow dance with her head nestled on his shoulder and her arms against his chest. Most of the couples had tears in their eyes, whispered sweet things and hugged each other tighter. After that evening, Mom went downhill so fast. The doctors suggested to Dad that she would need hospice care, and he flatly refused. He told them he would take care of 'His Sunny' until his dying breath!" Now openly sobbing, Ashley said, "He would bathe her, give her meds, dress her, change her bedding, try to feed her and carry her when it became necessary. It's not fair Danny! When we found Dad after he didn't answer the daily text system we had set up with him, I really broke down. Poor Andy didn't know how to comfort me."

"I know what you mean Sis. I went home and flopped down in my recliner with my head in my hands, my body shaking, trying not to cry. Maria knew instinctively what we must have found. She threw her arms around me for the longest time and gave me shoulder rubs and kisses. I think the worst part was finding Dad holding the two pictures in his lap of Mom with Chewie and the one of both of them with Braveheart. Then we found the locket clutched in his hand with their wedding picture inside. It's the one Mom never took off. She loved it so much. The doctors think he died of a broken heart, and I agree. They lived a long, very happy life, and I wouldn't have traded them for anyone else in the world. That was a pretty ingenious system they invented ahead of time for when Mom couldn't speak or move much of anything but her eyes, fingers and lips. What do you think of the story Dad told us about the day Mom passed away?"

Drying her eyes, Ashley said, "Well Danny, I absolutely believe it after hearing all their amazing stories about Chewie and then seeing firsthand for almost 15 years how incredibly intelligent Braveheart was. He understood complex English and knew things without any training whatsoever. He was almost suspiciously smart. When he looked at us with those big brown eyes, it was almost like he could read our minds and see right into our souls. Dad said that right before Mom passed, she pointed with her finger toward the picture of Chewie, and then she pointed toward the picture of Braveheart. Dad said he asked if she wanted to see the pictures closer, and she blinked the no signal. Then she pointed down toward the side of the bed on both sides and gave a slight smile. Dad suddenly knew what was going on. He asked if Chewie and Braveheart had come back to help her. She blinked the yes signal. Then she closed both eyes for about 10 seconds, which was their signal for I love you. He told her he would love her forever. Then she was gone, but she still had the slightest smile on her face. As you know, Dad was absolutely inconsolable and passed away just three days later. I pray daily that they meet again."

"Sis, I have to agree with you. I think it happened just like Dad said, and I pray we all meet again sometime. Hey, we have to shape up for when the rest of the gang get here. Recalling all that had me tearing up too. We can't be so depressed." Danny gave her a big bear hug and a smile.

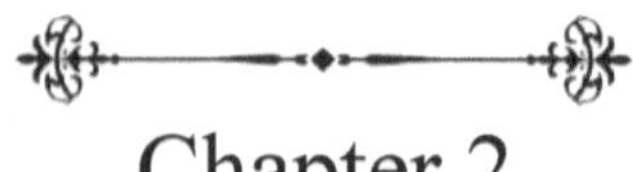

Chapter 2
Watching from Level 2, AKA, The Atonement Zone

Jim and Bill were looking down and observing what was happening with the Turner gang they had been protecting and subtly influencing over their many "down below" type years in the Atonement Zone. Bill was now in charge of this section of the Zone and had finally gotten Jim to beg El Jefe for forgiveness of his sins. It took many "down below" years to accomplish this, but it seemed like the blink of an eye when measured in Atonement Zone time. He was training Jim to take over for him when he would finally go to Level 1. Bill couldn't wait to see his wife and son again.

Jim said, "This is going to be a really sad day for all of them. It must have been a wild time for you Bill, when you were sent back by Johnnie, first as Chewie and then as Braveheart, to start protecting this wonderful family."

"You got that right, Jim! The bigger that family gets, the tougher it is to keep an eye on all of them. Those two sets of twins were the most difficult, especially when they were younger, as you well know. Sunny and BD were two of the finest people I ever knew, and I'm glad they went straight to Level 1. Johnnie tells me they did meet up again in a most wonderful, joyous reunion. But first they both independently made a stop at the 'Special Area' to spend time with Chewie and Braveheart for a while."

"Bill, were you responsible for sending Chewie and Braveheart back to help ease Sunny and BD along to Level 1?"

"Yes Jim, but Danny and Ashley don't know about me helping BD the same way as I did with Sunny."

"That's a wonderful thing you did Bill. I hope I can help people out like that someday."

"You will Jim, you're a good person. You already greatly helped this family on your way to Atonement and afterwards."

"Thanks Bill. By the way, when you talked to Johnnie, did you ever ask him what Level 1 is like?"

"Yes, I did once. He said it was a place of total peace, total love and mind bogglingly beautiful."

"Did he meet El Jefe, The Big Boss, or God? I still don't know what to call Him or Her or It."

"Jim, he said it was not so much a person, but a presence, a feeling of being wrapped in total forgiveness and love. It seems like it doesn't matter what term we use, as long as we believe."

"That is so awesome to know, Bill. Hey, check this out down below, another part of the Turner gang is arriving. It's Maria, Danny's wife and Andy, Ashley's hubby."

"Yep, and soon the gang of twins are going to be rolling or flying in from 4 different directions. Let's observe for a while and see if we can help make this whole gathering less somber. You're going to have to go back very soon. Old Stumpy will be waking up, and Dean wants to bring him /you along to the gathering. I think they may also bring Sheba."

"OK Bill, I sure love Ely and Dean. Their new child is the sweetest thing. They are so good to me, and I hate the thought of leaving them some day. Did you give any more thoughts to helping out Ely with a miracle?"

"Yes I did, stay tuned. Remember, you are going on 9 years old in 'down below dog years,' so maybe I can get you another 5 years. You are awfully old for such a big dog. I need you here to take over from me. Then I'll finally get to see my wife again. By the way, you and Sheba protect that beautiful child of theirs until then."

" OK Bill, see you soon. I may have a great idea for during their gathering and for when it starts to break up. I'll talk to you about it just before the gathering."

Chapter 3
The Rest of the Family

Maria spotted Andy pulling in at the postal center at the same time as her, and she gave him a wave. She noticed he was wearing his lieutenant's uniform and mentioned it. He told her that Chief Danny asked him to, so that no one would question them about spreading the ashes near the memorial bench. They could find no regulation prohibiting it, but it would look more professional this way with both wearing uniforms. As they walked the trail, they talked about how wonderfully they had been treated by Sunny and BD since day 1 of meeting them. Both agreed that they had also been truly blessed in their marriages. Maria was laughing about the time Danny stopped into the office and finally asked her out on a date. Then Andy told her about meeting Ashley, turning beet red and being tongue tied, so many years ago.

Maria said, "I still can't believe we both had a set of twins within a week of each other."

Andy laughed and replied, "That was peculiar and having them look so different, no identical twins for either of us. Twins don't run in either of our families. Of course, Sunny never even knew who her mom was, so it's possible. Can you imagine any mother giving up a beautiful child like Sunny must have been? She told us she had been dropped off in a box at a fire station in the middle of the night. God bless the foster parents who took her in and raised her to be such a wonderful person."

Maria's eyes flashed with anger just thinking about it. She couldn't imagine giving up a child under any circumstances.

"I think it's fantastic how wonderfully the 4 cousins get along together. They got especially tight after that crazy week back when they were all about 13 years old."

Andy said, "I can't believe we never had any more kids."

Maria blurted out, "It wasn't for lack of trying with Danny."

She cracked up when Andy turned red, and he finally said, "Ok, I also confess, me too. I mean, just look at Ashley, she is still gorgeous."

Danny and Ashley spotted them coming down the trail laughing like a couple of kids and were pleased that everyone in the family got along so well. They were a little surprised when they were greeted so passionately and kind of looked around to see if anyone else was walking on the trail.

Danny laughingly said, "Didn't we just see you guys this morning?"

Maria said, "Sure, but we really missed you both since then."

Ashley, with her arms tight around Andy, said, "We don't mind this type of greeting one little bit."

Danny, hugging Maria, said, "Copy that, let's do some more of this later!"

Danny got a notification on his special watch that his son Dean was about 5 miles away and would be there shortly. The very expensive watch was a gift from his son, who was in the genius category. He was an inventor and a multi-billionaire with numerous patents. The watch was almost weightless, flat and had a tiny screen. Danny saw the smiling face of his son and heard a "Hi Dad, see you soon."

Danny was so darn proud of him, but he couldn't remember if the patent for the watch that could do everything had been sold or not. The kid was into all kinds of things, and Danny didn't know how he kept track of it all. It makes his head spin when the kid tells him of the latest project he's working on.

Another notification came in from his daughter Christy, with her smiling face saying, "Daddy, I'm on the way."

It looked like she had her sharp looking SWAT uniform on. She was a lieutenant in the SWAT section of the police force, and Danny was so very proud of her for wanting to follow in his footsteps. She certainly had guts and literally no fear of any situation, but she also could show compassion when necessary. You couldn't have two children more different in looks for being twins. Christy is 5' 11" with black wavy hair and quite beautiful. Dean is about 5'7" with dark red hair and slender build. Christy had always been the protector in that pair. Dean had given her a locket with the same capability as his dad's watch, a tiny screen, speech capability, navigation, location to within inches and many other features. It was inscribed with "To the best Sis ever," and she loved it.

Suddenly, Ashley got a notification on her phone and projected it into a "Star Wars Like" three dimensional image. It was her beautiful daughter Soleada, who was another tiny strawberry blonde that looked just like Ashley and Sunny when they were that age. Everyone called her Lea. Lea waved and said, "Hi everyone, love y'all, and I'll be there shortly. I'm changing out of my nursing duds at the hospital. I should be there in 20 minutes."

Seconds later another beep sounded, and Ashley projected their son Ben in 3D. He gave a casual salute and yelled, "On the way Turner gang."

He was a plainclothes Detective 1st Grade under Danny's command and was a head taller than his sister Lea. He was good looking, with wavy black hair like his dad. He had been the protector in that pair growing up and still worries about Lea's safety to this very day. Lea liked to tease him about being a mother hen.

Everyone in the family were either cops or nurses except for Maria and Dean, and Sunny and BD had been so proud of them all, never showing favoritism to any of them. Dean was the odd twin out and was considered a little eccentric by many people, but he had one of the highest IQs ever measured. He was a philanthropist and one of the richest people in the country, but he was still just a down to earth, all around good person. Considering the bullying he had endured in his youth, he had still kept his sense of humor and kindness to everyone. He had secretly paid for all of his grandma and grandpas' huge medical bills and had set his parents up for continuous care for life if ever needed. He offered his sister and two cousins money to help pay for their houses, but they all thanked him and declined the generous offers.

He just said, "If ever you need me, I'm here for you. I will never, ever forget how you helped me when we were young."

They all said, "We love you, IQ," using his nickname he had acquired when in grade school.

Chapter 4
The Rough Years for Dean

Dean was a short, skinny kid with glasses and wild red hair sticking out in all directions in grade school. He was bullied, pushed around and called all kinds of names but only when his two cousins and sister weren't around. They called him carrot top, Howdy Doody, freak and even "red on the noodle like the balls on a poodle." The bullying slowed down to a trickle when Christy picked up and slammed one of the biggest bullies against a locker so hard that it dented the locker and knocked the wind out of the kid.

She grabbed him by the collar and said, "Final warning, you punkass!" and dropped him on his back on the floor. She later got called to the principal's office for a meeting with him and her dad.

The principal knew what had been going on, and there were no repercussions. He just smiled and said, "Try not to hurt that punk too badly. By the way, did you know that you and your brother have the highest grades in the entire class with your two cousins close behind, and you have never once been in trouble. I wish I had more kids like you."

Christy thought she would be grounded for life, but her dad just hugged her on the way out and said he was so proud of her for sticking up for her brother.

It was in 6th grade when Dean came into his own. School was so easy for him that the teachers all thought he could skip grades or even go right into college, but he didn't want to change a thing. After all, his two cousins and sister were in the same grade. The teachers all decided to let him do whatever studying in class that he wanted, since he blew through every test with an A+ without fail. He would read about advanced electronics, physics and thermodynamics. He asked to take the college boards just for fun and had gotten the highest scores possible. He had his first invention in 6th grade and got a patent on it. He had miniaturized a drone to the size of a horsefly which could stay aloft for an hour. It had a micro battery, and it could record photos and videos on a chip so small it could barely be seen. He had secretly been offered a huge sum of money by the government for the patent and also a standing job offer after high school or college. He kept exclusive rights to manufacture the drone, but it would only be produced for the government. This had made him a mutimillionaire, but he wanted to keep it a secret for as long as possible. He had his dad invest the money for him in various safe, diversified funds.

There was also another reason he wanted to stay in the same grade, and her name was Elyssia Simmons. She had transferred to this school and was totally without friends. She was shunned by the girls because of her birth defect, a left hand missing the pinky and ring finger. She was very pretty with thick, wavy blonde hair and big blue eyes, and Dean was in puppy love for the first time in his life. No other guys were interested in her because of her hand. She was sitting alone at lunch as usual and looking very depressed when Dean went over to introduce himself and offered to help her catch up with her studies. He said they could study at his house, and he would quickly get her up to speed. He called her Miss Ely, and she was astounded that he never once stared at her hand or made fun of her.

She said, "I would really like that, IQ. Oh God, is it ok to call you that?"

"Of course Miss Ely, it's true, I was blessed with a pretty good brain."

From that day forward they were close friends, and Dean would carry her computer and the very few books that were still in use as they walked to his house. They were only about to be bullied one time, but the guy had second thoughts when he looked around and saw Christy walking behind them. He was still scared of her because of the way she stared at him in class. He took off in the other direction and didn't bother them again.

Dean could speak 6 languages fluently and knew the answers to just about everything. As they walked along he would sometimes talk to Ely in French and teach her words and phrases, and she would just stare at him in awe. Whenever they saw a dog, he knew everything about it, no matter what breed it was. He confided to her that he had always wanted a dog, but his dad was reluctant to let him have one. He thought that possibly it was because his dad was worried that they would never find one as smart as Braveheart. He remembered how his grandparents would often eat at the old Thai restaurant downtown just to have an excuse to stop in at the animal shelter and check out the dogs. They never could find one that even remotely measured up to Chewie or Braveheart.

Dean's mom, Maria, liked sweet Ely from the start and never once mentioned her hand. She thought they made a cute couple. When she found out Ely was from a broken home with an abusive father who had left her mother when Ely was very young, her heart went out to her. She remembered the story of Sunny and how she was given up at birth. She vowed to treat Ely as if she was her own child. Maria noticed that whenever Dean got up to get a drink for the two of them or get some study supplies, Ely's hands would go across her heart, and she would tilt her head and watch Dean with a look of total fascination.

When Ely mentioned that she had a birthday coming up in another week, Maria grabbed Dean by the arm later that day and said, "Can't you see that Ely absolutely adores you?"

Dean looked bewildered and said, "She does?"

Maria said, "Oh my God, you men, you better get her something really, really nice!"

"Ok Mom, I'll take care of everything! I've been working on a project just like that, and it will be perfect." Dean made a quick call to some top employees of his in the new company he had just started, called "Microdots," and told them what he wanted.

With the help of his dad, some of his patent millions, and a lot of hard work, the small company was a very successful miniaturization marvel. Dean would only hire eccentric geniuses for the top positions. He didn't care what they looked like or how they dressed. The team was extremely loyal and would do anything to please him. Dean paid them extremely well, had after work parties for their families and made it a fun place to work.

On the day of Ely's birthday he got permission to treat the entire class to pizza, sodas and cake, and even some of the girls started to come around and talk to her.

As they walked to Dean's house, he casually held her hand and got real close to her, almost arm in arm. When they walked into the house, Ely was shocked when she saw all the Turner gang was there, and they started yelling, "Surprise!"

There were balloons, decorations, presents and a huge birthday cake. Ely started to tear up and told them she never had a party before.

Then Dean gave her his gift, and she slowly opened the elaborately wrapped, felt lined box. Inside was a locket made of white gold coated with rhodium, one of the most expensive metals for jewelry. It was engraved with "Ely and IQ, Best Friends For Life"

Ely started sobbing, and IQ said, "I'm sorry, Ely, I can get you something else."

Ely grabbed him and kissed him right on the lips. "These are happy tears IQ. I absolutely love it. Nobody was ever as nice to me as you and your family! Please put it around my neck."

Maria gave Dean two thumbs up and winked. Dean smiled and started to explain something else about the locket. It had a secret latch that opened to a small engraved picture of the two of them taken by Maria while they were huddled close together studying. It also had a miniature call button that would activate IQ's phone messaging system if she ever needed help. He had already paid for lifetime satellite phone messaging. It was a technological wonder and had a couple of other secret things it could do. Those he would show her later.

Ely grabbed him in a bear hug while the tears flowed. Like most guys, he didn't know what to do or say. After a while, he told her not to mention the secret call button to anyone, but she could show the other girls in class the picture if she wanted to. Ely hugged and thanked everyone profusely and told them it was the absolute best day of her life.

Dean seemed to have only one guy in the class that he still had trouble with. The kid was an oversized bully, but he was the best athlete by far. He had been recruited to play Junior Varsity football as a tight end even at that young age. Dean watched a couple of games and noticed how the kid could be a standout at the next game if he followed his plan. The coach wouldn't give Dean the time of day, thinking a little guy like that wouldn't know anything about a rough contact sport. Dean decided to approach the bully directly. Surprisingly, big Joe Hill, the bully, actually listened to Dean after he heard the plan. Dean told him he observed that the top defender on the next team they were to play was left handed and was considerably slower to react when he had to cover a receiver who cut to his right side. He told Joe to go downfield, cut a sharp left and leave the guy flatfooted. He said the coach wouldn't listen to his plan and to set it up with the quarterback. The plan worked to perfection with Joe scoring twice and having 155 total yards receiving. The coach yelled at him for not running the called routes but grudgingly had to admit the plan worked. When he found out it was Dean who designed the play, he asked him and Joe to come to his office.

He said, "Well, do you two have any other tricks up your sleeves for the next game when we play the undefeated Red Rock Raiders?"

Dean said, "Yes Sir, as a matter of fact we do."

Joe stared at Dean like he had antlers. Dean suggested that the coach resurrect the very old, no longer used single wing formation with the ball centered directly to Joe and run a couple of plays to the left. He told him that Joe not only was powerful enough to get some running first downs, but he had a great arm. He said they should run the next series of plays to the right and pass to their quickest receiver way downfield. The other team would be expecting another run, and the play should work. The coach thought about it and had the team practice it inside the gym totally in private. Since he had some very good blocking linemen, the coach came up with a few more plays utilizing Joe and the single wing formation. On game day the plays worked to perfection, and they defeated the Raiders by 3 points. After that day all bullying stopped, and Joe would give Dean a fist bump whenever he saw him in the halls. Joe told all the guys and girls in the class that bullying of anyone would not be tolerated. Dean became a regular consultant for the coach with great success.

Chapter 5
The Secrets Out

Somehow word leaked out about Dean, his Microdots Company and the fact that he was worth many millions. He suddenly was getting quite a bit of attention from the girls in the class, much to Ely's consternation. Dean very politely turned all of them down and said he already had a very special lady. The guys were all kind of jealous, but they knew he only had eyes for Ely. Dean treated everyone nicely, especially the ones who had trouble fitting in. A couple of them eventually were hired by him after graduation and were very devoted employees.

Danny and Maria were more than a little worried about Dean drawing too much attention, so Danny had some of his officers keep watch from a distance before and after school. He also turned down frequent requests from news organizations asking to interview Dean. Dean said he could easily handle any of them and their questions, but he could see how worried his parents were, so he respected their decisions.

There were two very bad characters who had been following the news, and they were trying to come up with a foolproof plan of parting a lot of that money from Dean and his company. They had just been released from the Federal Prison near The Villages after serving 5 years for drug offenses and violent crimes against women. The ringleader was named Wallace Schmidt and was 6' 3", weighing about 275 pounds. His partner was a smaller guy named Cory Hills and was about 5' 9", weighing about 165 pounds. He had been protected in prison by Wallace and would do anything he was told to do. They both could find only low paying janitorial and landscaping jobs, which they hated. They vowed to study the situation and follow the daily movements of Dean. They drove a beat up, ancient gas powered white van. They followed Dean several times and some hot little blonde who was always with him. Cory was very much interested in the blonde, but Wallace gave him a few whacks, told him she was only about 12 or 13 years old and to concentrate on the money. Cory thought to himself that he would grab the blond too if he got a chance. They noticed they were being followed by cops in a cruiser a couple of times and had to turn onto side streets so that it wasn't obvious what they were up to. They would bide their time and hopefully find a way to grab the kid off the street and hold him for ransom. They needed to find a safe hideout, a method to get the ransom and a method to get away safely. They also needed some burner phones and a second vehicle. They could possibly try to obtain a weapon. Guns were now highly restricted and regulated, but Cory knew a guy who could probably get his hands on one. They didn't want to rush this operation and end up back in prison. A lot more planning was in order.

Bill was watching these two characters from up in the Level Two Atonement Zone and didn't like what he was seeing. He had to come up with a plan to protect Dean and of course, his cute girlfriend. He was racking his brain for a way to do it. "Think Bill, Think!" Finally he developed a rather complicated plan involving lots of different players. He decided to recall Jim from down below where he was being punished and had not yet achieved atonement.

Poor Jim happened to be a seal on a large ice floe that day, and he was being attacked by killer whales. They were trying to wash him off the floe by making waves stream across the floe using their bodies and flukes. Jim was barely holding on when "poof," he was back up to Level 2, the Atonement Zone.

Jim was still shaking with fear when he saw Bill. "Bill, what happened? I thought for sure those killer whales were going to get me and have a nice lunch!"

"Jim, I need you here to watch a couple of very bad actors. We have to protect IQ and Ely from them. I'm going to give you two last assignments, and both of them will be on dry land for a change. Make sure you don't blow this assignment!"

"Only two more, Bill? Thank you, I won't let you down. I understand why I was being punished all this time."

Bill still hadn't gotten Jim to beg for forgiveness from El Jefe, the Big Boss, or God as many religions call Him (or Her or It). He thought these last two assignments would do the trick. "Jim, you will have to be really sharp to pull this off, and I plan to give you some assistance from another section of the zone up here in Level 2."

"Another section Bill?"

"Yes Jim, you didn't think you were the only one having to atone for your sins, did you? Her name is Victoria or Vickie, for short. She has already attained atonement, and this is her final assignment before going to Level 1. You will be working together after you complete the first one of the two assignments. Vickie, come on over and meet Jim."

"Hello Jim, I'm Vickie."

"Hi Vickie, congratulations on attaining atonement." Jim was very impressed with Vickie, a very attractive brunette. He wondered in what form she would be going back down below?

"Thanks Jim, hopefully we can also get you there. Bill says this next one for you will be difficult, but I have no idea yet of what we need to do. I'll see you later." Just like that, she was gone and over in her own section of the zone.

Chapter 6
Jim's First of the Final Two Atonement Tests

Bill had Jim observe a desolate area near a lake in Florida, one of the few big lakes, surrounded by about 50 acres of old orange trees and pasture, that The Villages didn't own. There were huge oak trees, magnolias, pines and bald cypress trees completely hiding a small 2 room cabin with a back door leading to the water's edge and a small hidden dock. An old rowboat was attached to the dock. There were several run down kennels along the side of the cabin where two guys ran an illegal pit bull breeding business. Slim and Big Sam were the very definition of rednecks. They would sell the pit bulls to dog fighting rings for a good buck. Business was getting slower and slower as more and more dog fighting rings were being shut down, and the perpetrators were being arrested for animal cruelty. They were down to one pitbull, a very large pregnant female named Sadie that they had grabbed off the streets as a stray. They didn't know who the father was, but they had high hopes the puppies would be mean, large, purebred and valuable. Poor Sadie had a huge, 15 foot long heavy chain attached to her collar and to an eyebolt on the old wooden cage with the broken door. She was underfed, unloved and barely had enough water to sustain her pregnancy.

In another of the cages was a very unusual gigantic cat. It was supposed to be a Maine Coon cat or a Norwegian Forest cat, but it was way larger than either of them. This totally black cat was a female and weighed at least 40 to 45 pounds with yellow eyes and a mean disposition. They had also found her on the streets as a younger stray. She was a freak of nature, and the guys thought they could throw her in against a pitbull for a fun fight. They could possibly make some great cash betting for her, rather than for a pitbull who they would choose for being less aggressive and smaller than a normal one.

"Bill, these two guys are real pricks! Who would keep dogs and cats in those conditions and come up with a horrible plan like that? I hate those bastards!"

"Well Jim, you can do something about that. This is where you get your first of the two last assignments. So don't blow it! Don't make me look bad!"

"Bill, wait, what is my assignment and what do I do?"

"Jim, I told you earlier, protect IQ and Ely with your life if necessary. You are going back now as Sadie."

"Bill, wait, what the Hell, I mean Heck! But she's a female!"

"Ok, Captain Obvious. Now back you go."

Suddenly, Jim was in the cage and feeling very uncomfortable as Sadie.

"Seriously Bill, no male parts and I'm fat as a house! Something is moving inside me!"

"Yep Jim, get ready to experience your feminine side and protect all 7 of those puppies."

"Seven? You mean I have to have 7 puppies? Why don't you just send me back as that seal on the ice floe? Isn't this going to really hurt?"

Now Jim had Bill laughing out loud. "Sorry, but this is important. Maybe you will appreciate more of what females of all species have to go through."

Slim suddenly appeared out of the shack carrying some cheap dog food and a jug of water. He hated that Big Sam made him feed and fill the water bowls of any animals that they had, while the big slob sat in the cabin drinking a cup of coffee with his feet propped up. He poured water in Sadie's bowl and dumped a pile of dog food right on the floor of the cage. He noticed Sadie was about to give birth and hoped for a bumper crop of big, tough, strong puppies. Even though Sadie was laying down panting, she forced herself to eat and drink. The cheap dog food tasted like cardboard to Jim, but he needed it for his babies.

"Oh great, now he was thinking like a mother!"

Slim very carefully fed and sloshed water into the cage where the freak cat was housed. This cat scared the heck out of him ever since they grabbed her up off the street. She would hiss and try to claw or bite anyone who came near her. She would glare at him with those yellow eyes and open her mouth showing large razor sharp teeth. They named her Sheba and put a tag on the cage in case any of their sleazy group of fellow dog fighting ring friends were interested in purchasing her. Sheba hated that dog food and wanted real meat, but she had to eat something to survive.

Suddenly, Vickie found herself inside Sheba and complained to Bill up in Level 2. "Are you kidding me Bill, a black cat in a cramped cage in this Florida heat? I thought I would have an easy assignment after achieving atonement."

"Sorry Vickie, I need you to help Jim achieve atonement, and it is very complicated. I also need you to help protect IQ and Ely. You are one big, beautiful cat if I may say so! You will have a life of luxury soon if all goes according to plan."

"Jim, is that you inside Sadie? This plan is nuts. What do you know about having babies?"

"I guess I'll just go with the flow and let Sadie do all the work. By the way, Bill is right, you are the most beautiful cat I've ever seen! Those golden yellow eyes and jet black fur are just amazing. You are also beautiful in person."

"Well thanks Jim, I'll give it my best shot at helping you."

Slim went back into the cabin and told Big Sam about Sadie looking like she was about to give birth. Big Sam just told him to check it out every hour.

Chapter 7
Atonement Day

It was a Sunday, and the 4 Turner cousins would all get together along with Ely, who was now an honorary member of the gang, for fun and games. The gang convinced IQ to go along on a fishing expedition to that same hidden lake even though he would rather work on one of his many inventions. Although his company had plenty of work scheduled, IQ shut down on most Sundays in case any of his workers wanted to attend church services. He often thought about religion, a higher power and whether there was a need to attend any fancy churches with all the rigamarole. He decided he would pray by himself and with Miss Ely, as he decided there was indeed someone or something looking out for the Turner family. He mostly prayed that good things would happen for Miss Ely, who had such a rough start in life. The gang suggested he bring along some of his newest drones and test fly them out over the lake. The lake was about 8 miles from their homes, and they decided to take the E-Scooters which had some serious upgrades put on by IQ. These big-tired scooters could haul up to 250 pounds of riders and freight and achieve speeds up to 40mph. IQ had added navigation screens, lights, turn signals and long distance solid state batteries.

Ely rode behind IQ with her arms around him and her head looking over his shoulder, a situation which he really enjoyed. Ely would give his cheek a smooch every so often, and he could hardly concentrate on his driving. Ely had never been so happy in her entire life since meeting IQ at school, and the rest of the family were so nice to her. Beautiful Lea brought along her first aid and trauma kit since she was an intern for the summer at her mom's hospital. Ben, a summer intern and "gofer" at the police headquarters, brought along the newest 3 foot long, electric shock stick which could knock a big man out easily. Christy brought a large, almost certainly illegal, 8" switchblade which she had honed the edges as sharp as a razor blade. She also interned at the police headquarters and had found that blade in an unused desk drawer. IQ had his newest drones in a large backpack in the carrier basket. All the fishing equipment was strapped to Christy's basket. They made quick time to the lake down a couple of very narrow dirt roads and trails only they knew about. They ended up at the far side of the lake directly across from the hidden cabin. After they parked the scooters and got their fishing equipment ready, IQ scanned the water and banks for gators. He got out his mid-sized drone and showed Ely how to operate it. She was always amazed at his intelligence and listened intently to everything he said. IQ gave the ok to fish to the others, but told them to stay back at least 10' from the water's edge and watch out for gators, especially if they hooked a fish. The splashing and commotion could easily attract a big gator. After he and Ely sent up the mid-sized drone and took it out halfway across the lake, he rotated the high definition camera around and discovered the cabin and dock, which none of them knew existed. It was at least a half mile across the lake. Looking on the screen and zooming in they noticed the kennels. The cabin was rundown, and it looked like no one was there, but they discovered that two of the kennels were occupied, one with a dog and the other with what looked like a small black panther. They noticed that the dog was in some kind of distress and laying there gasping in obvious pain.

Ely said, "IQ, I think that dog is going to give birth."

"Ely, I think you're right. This might be part of the last dog fighting ring in the whole area, and whoever lives there is breeding and selling them. Dad warned us about that possibility and that they might be dangerous. Let's keep watch with the drone. It still has a good 70% battery life. We can always notify my dad later. Let's show the others."

IQ called out to the others to come over and decided to fly over a little closer. He was able to get to within a hundred yards and a much better view. They were right, the dog had just given birth to a tiny puppy. In a short time another one was born. Since Christy was a cat lover who had always wanted a kitty and had asked her dad several times for one, IQ zoomed in on the cage with Sheba in it. Christy was fascinated.

"Oh guys, she's beautiful, look how big! She must be over 40 pounds. Why do they have her and why in such a small cage?"

IQ said that he thought they possibly might want her to fight.

Christy said, "That's awful, we have to do something. I would love that cat for a pet. Let's call Dad, he'll know what to do."

"Christy, let's wait a little and observe, just in case they are legitimate owners."

By this time Sadie had delivered 6 puppies, but something looked off about them.

They all had some type of deformity, either missing an ear, had bulging eyes or had crooked mouth alignments. The last puppy was giving Sadie a very hard time and a tremendous amount of pain. When it finally came out, it was three times bigger than the others and had its eyes wide open. It was missing its front left paw, but otherwise looked very normal, but nothing like a pitbull. It was going to be huge. It even had its "milk teeth" already and could walk a little, but with a limp. This puppy was very unusual, and IQ had a premonition about it.

Ely had tears in her eyes and told IQ, "We have to save them." She was rubbing her own left hand without realizing it. "I would really like to have that big one IQ, but my mom would never let me. I would take such good care of it."

Suddenly, the cabin door opened, and Slim started out toward the kennels. IQ quickly pulled the drone back to 200 yards where it couldn't be heard or easily seen. Slim was surprised to see the puppies and was shocked when he saw they were all deformed. He whacked on the pen and cursed out Sadie for a good 5 minutes.

Jim said, "Bill, that was really painful, but I love all my babies. I have to clean them off and get them to nurse. I can't believe how wonderful it is to have babies and the love I feel for them. Oh Vickie, look how cute they are!"

"They sure are, but be careful of those two bastards Jim. They can't be trusted."

Jim cleaned and nudged all the babies over to nurse, letting Sadie's natural maternal instinct take over. He especially took note that Slim cursed out the biggest one and blamed him for the rest being deformed. Jim/Sadie loved that big one the most.

Slim headed in to give Big Sam the bad news. He was going to be really pissed off.

Big Sam came out of the cabin uttering vile curses that would even make a sailor blush. When he got to the cage and saw the puppies, he got even more enraged. He was ready to beat Sadie, but he calmed down slightly when Slim convinced him that they could breed her again, this time to a normal pit bull.

"Damn it Slim, get a burlap bag and throw all the puppies in it. Tie the top off and chuck them as far out in the lake as you can. They'll go down faster than a fat kid on a seesaw." He was a sadistic SOB and was laughing about his own joke. He headed back into the cabin for a shot of the Jack Daniels he had stashed away.

Slim hated this idea and knew it was the worst type of animal abuse, but he couldn't go up against Big Sam. He reluctantly went searching in the shed, but he could only find a large 45 gallon contractor plastic bag. He decided to use that and just poke a couple of holes in it with his jackknife.

Both Jim and Vickie had heard the conversation and were outraged.

"Vickie, they are going to kill my beautiful babies. What can we do?"

"Damn them to Level 3! If only I could get this cage open, I could tear them to shreds. I'm so sorry Jim."

"I have to try to protect my babies. Maybe I can get this chain loose." Sadie pulled as hard as she could, but the collar was too tight around her neck. She carefully pushed the babies aside and walked to the back of the old wooden pen and chewed at the wood around the eyebolt. If only she had more time. The biggest puppy was watching her intently the whole time while the other 6, eyes still closed, aimlessly searched for her.

Slim arrived back at the cage with his bag and reached through the back of the pen looping Sadie's chain over a large bent nail. She could no longer get back to her puppies. He opened the pen's flimsy front door and started grabbing the puppies one by one and tossing them in the bag. The biggest freak actually tried to bite him, something he never would have guessed could occur at that age. He finally grabbed it by the back of its neck and tossed him in last. All the while Sadie tried desperately to get loose.

"Vickie, he's taking my babies. Oh God, don't let him drown my babies!"

Sheba started screeching and banging all around her cage like a maniac, trying to get the latch open. Slim glanced over at her nervously and wondered what was wrong with her to act up like that. That crazy cat bitch, they should have never picked her up off the streets. She's been nothing but trouble. He tied the bag closed and headed for the lake.

IQ said, "Oh no, they are going to drown the puppies in the lake. I have them recorded on sound as well as video. Christy, quick get the biggest drone out of my backpack."

As Slim approached the lake, he got out his jackknife but heard something approaching from the sky. IQ had zoomed in quickly and activated the speaker. "We see you and are recording everything. Put down the bag. We have notified the police."

Now Slim was in a panic. This was not good. He knew there were really strict laws against all their activities. He peered way across the lake and saw what looked like 5 kids. He decided to finish the job, get Big Sam and go after the kids and their evidence.

Sadie was lunging against the chain and managed to bend the nail over. She charged for the door of the pen and pulled the eyebolt out of the old wooden slat she had been chewing on. Slim heard the noise, saw her coming and decided he didn't have time to slit the bag, so he threw it far out into the lake. It would sink eventually. Slim picked up the big lid from a 45 gallon metal garbage can to defend himself from Sadie. Instead of charging for him, she went running toward the lake thinking she could save her babies.

Slim hollered at Sadie, "Stop, you crazy bitch, the chain is too heavy!"

Meanwhile Vickie was still screeching and going crazy in her cage and starting to bend the metal latch of the door. She said, "Jim, don't do it, your chain is way too heavy."

Jim said, "I have to swim out and bring my babies back. I can't let them drown. Mama's coming for you, babies!"

He plunged into the lake and started swimming toward the bag. He begged Bill up in Level 2 for help, but he got no response. After he got within 5 feet of the bag, the heavy chain pulled him under, and a couple of minutes later he was back in Level 2. Poor Sadie had drowned.

"No Bill, No, No, No! My babies, save my babies!"

There was no response, so Jim started praying fervently to El Jefe, God, the Big Boss. "Please Jefe, please God, save my babies! They are just innocent little babies. Please, please forgive me for all my sins down on earth. I don't care if you punish me for a hundred more years, but please save my babies!"

Bill suddenly came back and said, "Now Jim, that is exactly what El Jefe wanted to hear you say! Watch what happens down below."

Jim started watching the action with a look of total anguish on his face. He kept sending up silent prayers to Level 1 constantly, begging for El Jefe to save his babies.

Chapter 8
Close Call for the Kids

The Turner kids and Ely had watched the whole episode and were determined to save the puppies. IQ deployed his largest drone, and it was outfitted as a delivery drone in the testing stages with 3 automatic hooks to carry packages or food. He told Ely to bring back the smaller drone, and she just got it to shore in time before the battery ran out. He told her to remove the memory cards and hide them in her pockets. He quickly sent the large drone up and flew to the floating garbage bag. It took him about a minute to latch onto the knotted part with a hook, and he started to tow it towards their side of the lake. It was heavy and slow going to start, but his drone was at 100% charge and would have juice to spare. He told Ben to call the Police Headquarters and report the whole situation, their exact location and that they would need help. He told Christy and Lea to get the E-Scooters ready to go and leave the fishing equipment there. They would have to leave as soon as he got the bag to shore.

Slim shook his head at the stupid dog, Sadie, for drowning like that and knew Big Sam would be furious. He headed for the cabin just as Sheba bent the latch enough to force her way out of the cage. She was sprinting towards him like a demon from Level 3, screeching and hissing all the way.

Vickie was enraged, "You killed my friend, you son of a bitch! I'll tear you a new asshole!"

Luckily he still had the garbage can lid, as it took him all his strength to fight off the crazy cat bitch and make it inside the door of the cabin. Big Sam had been napping the whole time with a half empty booze bottle beside him. He certainly came awake fast enough when Slim told him what had transpired outside. A string of loud, filthy curses filled the air as he told Slim to pack all their meager belongings into their beat up old pickup truck. They would drive around to the other side of the lake and get any evidence from those kids, one way or the other. He couldn't believe what he was seeing, a heavy bag full of evidence against them now moving quickly towards the other shore. Those damn kids were using a big drone!

Sheba ran to the water's edge and grabbed the end of the 15' heavy chain with her teeth and started to pull with all her strength. She managed to get the chain moving with great effort and finally pulled Sadie to the edge of the lake. She pulled Sadie about 15' up the bank by her collar, but screeched in sadness and anger when she saw she couldn't help her.

Vickie said, "Bill, why did you let that happen?"

Bill replied, "Vickie, Jim is here with me, and you'll meet up again soon. Please stay there until the police arrive. There will be a girl named Christy coming along who wants you for her kitty. She will treat you wonderfully, and no one will ever hurt you again. Be very nice to the whole gang of Turner cousins and to Miss Ely. They are very good people and are trying to save Sadie's puppies. By the way, Jim has finally achieved atonement."

Vickie didn't respond and just lay there with her front legs over Sadie giving out low wailing and sad moaning sounds. She would protect Sadie's body until help came. The splashing and noises had attracted the attention of an 8 foot gator who started slowly cruising over that way in hopes of a nice easy meal.

Big Sam and Slim got the truck loaded and knew they had limited time to drive to the other side of the lake, catch those damn brats and collect the evidence. They would have to leave the area as soon as possible after that and the deserted cabin they had been squatting in for free. Big Sam was furious, and he decided they might have to silence those kids for ruining his operation. It would take 10-15 minutes to follow the narrow winding dirt roads to the other side and maybe 20 minutes for the cops to show up. It was going to be a close call. He gunned the old truck and branches were hitting all sides as they followed the bumpy, curving dirt road.

IQ had maneuvered the bag to shore, and they secured it to Lea's scooter and transferred her first aid equipment to Ben's scooter. He opened the top of the bag to let air into the puppies. He told Lea to start down the narrowest path with the puppies and don't stop. He would follow behind with Ely and have Ben and Christy bring up the rear. They could dump off the medium sized drone as a distraction, and maybe it would make Slim and Big Sam think they had found the video and voice recorder evidence. They all took off and were almost seen by the guys as the truck came around the corner into the clearing where they had been fishing. Slim jumped out of the truck and looked around the area. He quickly spotted the abandoned fishing equipment. He searched around and finally found the narrow trail with the scooter wheel tracks showing. Fat Big Sam just kept his lazy ass planted in the truck, and Slim knew he would have to do all the dirty work if they wanted to avoid jail time. He thought the narrow trails crossed the dirt road at one point about a mile from there. If they could get there in time, they could cut those punk kids off. He jumped back into the truck and told Big Sam to haul ass to the crossing.

The kids were going as fast as they could on the narrow, bumpy winding paths, and Lea with the puppies and IQ with Ely reached the crossing and hustled over into the next trail. Ben and Christy could hear the revved up truck coming in the distance and flew across the road just in time. Christy's scooter hit a root and threw her off about 150 feet down the narrow trail. She was ok, with just a skinned knee, but she was shaken up, and Ben quickly came up with a plan. He stopped, hid his scooter behind a very large palmetto bush, grabbed the drone off Christy's scooter and threw it out onto the trail. He helped Christy up and told her the plan. She would lay back down, make believe she was injured, and Ben would hide behind the palmetto. The truck came to a sliding stop, and Slim jumped out. He had a leer on his face as he walked toward the drone and saw Christy on the ground. As usual, Big Sam stayed in the truck.

Slim grabbed the drone and said, "You little bitch, where is the bag with the puppies? I'll let you go if you hand them over." He had no such idea, since she could identify him to the cops.

Christy jumped up and pressed the button on the huge, dual edge switchblade, flicking it open and saying, "Come and get them, asshole!"

Slim debated with himself for a moment, as all he had was his little jackknife. He had a lot more muscle and weight, but he would have to be very careful. He knew a knife like that could be very dangerous. Big Sam was watching from the truck and grinning like an idiot. He loved to watch fighting as long as he wasn't involved. Christy stood her ground, waving the big blade back and forth. As Slim got within 10 feet, he passed the palmetto, and that was the last thing he remembered for 15 minutes. Ben had activated the three foot long shock stick and set it to maximum. He jammed it into Slim's side, and it knocked him back three feet and out cold. Big Sam couldn't believe what he was seeing, and he decided to cut and run, leaving Slim to take the blame. He peeled out down the dirt road intending to get as far away as possible and hide out somewhere.

Ben and Christy got back on their scooters and headed down the path where they met up with IQ, Lea and Ely. They quickly told them what happened.

Ben said, "IQ, your sister is one badass and will make a great cop!"

Christy was grinning, and said, "Ditto for you, cousin Ben! As Grandpa BD would say, 'We showed them where the bear shit in the buckwheat'!"

As all this was happening, the police had activated every SWAT team in the entire county, and they were soon swarming toward the lake and the hidden cabin. IQ had given them their exact location and shortly a three man SWAT drone swooped down to land near them. As luck would have it, IQ and Christy's Dad, Chief Danny Turner, was in it. He jumped out and silently thanked God that they were all ok. They quickly filled him in on everything, and Christy saw her big chance.

Christy said, "Daddy, we need to rescue the kitty who tried to help save the dog and her puppies. She is still at the cabin. Could you please take me along to get her? Daddy, I never, ever ask you for anything, but could I please keep the kitty? I'll take complete care of her. You and Mom won't have to do anything."

Chief Danny was so relieved that all the kids were ok that he said, "Ok honey, I know you have wanted one for a long time." He told Christy to hop in the drone and left one officer to watch over the kids and make sure they got home ok.

IQ arranged for the puppies to get sent to a vet and then to a no kill shelter in town. He called the shelter to arrange for special feeding and care for the puppies. IQ was a big contributor to the shelter, and they would do whatever they could to save them. Ely was very quiet on the way home, and IQ wondered if she was ok or in shock. He finally said when they got home, "Miss Ely, are you ok?"

"IQ, is there any way we could keep that big puppy with the missing front left paw? I just have a feeling he's going to be very special." She looked at IQ, and her big blue eyes were starting to get moist with tears. IQ had heard her at the lake and saw her rubbing her own left hand in sympathy with the big puppy. He also couldn't resist her when she looked at him that way.

"Let me talk to Daddy. I never ask him for anything. I think he will OK it, especially after agreeing to let Christy have that massive cat that she told him was just a kitty. I wish we could see his face when he gets to the cabin." Ely gave IQ a big kiss and hug and told him she would get a babysitting job or something to help pay for the care of the dog. She even knew some neighbors that wanted someone to pull weeds and run errands.

He laughed and said, "Miss Ely, we have plenty of money, no need to ever worry about that. He will be our dog after we get married anyway. I loved you from the first day I saw you in the cafeteria and we walked home together. I would do anything for you!"

It was then that the big blue eyes opened up with tears. "Oh IQ, I love you so much. Please tell me you aren't kidding."

"I'm not kidding Miss Ely, but let's keep it our little secret for now. We'll check in at the shelter tomorrow and see how he's doing. I'll talk to Daddy tonight. I also had a strong feeling about that dog." Ely was beyond happy. She couldn't stop thinking about the future!

The drone with Christy, her Dad and the SWAT officer arrived at the cabin at the same time as two other teams. They secured the cabin area as Christy pointed out the area of the lake where the puppies were tossed. They found Sheba guarding Sadie's body and keeping an 8' foot gator at bay with hissing open jaws, razor sharp claws and arched back.

Chief Danny got out his own taser type shock stick and gave the gator a mild shock sending it back into the lake.

Danny looked at Christy and said, "That's the so-called kitty? It's as big as a bloody small panther! Be careful, she may be dangerous!"

"Oh Daddy, she's just been mistreated. Let me talk to her. Her cage said her name was Sheba."

"Sheba, come here. My name is Christy, and I'm so sorry we couldn't save your friend. We saved her puppies, and they are at the vet right now. If you will be my kitty, I'll take great care of you, and nobody will ever hurt you again."

Vickie remembered what Bill up in Level 2 told her and instantly relaxed. She slinked over to Christy and rubbed up against her, letting herself be petted. She could feel the love radiating from Christy.

"Oh Daddy, she is even more beautiful than I thought. We will get her the best food and a big soft bed. Oh my, she will need a really big sandbox too.”

Danny had never seen his daughter so happy, but wow, what a huge cat. He wondered what his wife would say.

“Oh Sheba, you have a cut on your shoulder. Don’t worry, my cousin is a nurse and will fix you right up. You will love my whole family and also Ely. Will you be good and come home with me?”

Vickie decided to nod three times, just like the dogs that she had heard about, Chewie and Braveheart.

“Oh my God Daddy, did you see that? She nodded yes.”

“I did Christy, could she possibly understand us?”

Vickie nodded three times again. This was going to be fun.

“Let’s keep this a secret for now. We have to decide what to do with Sadie.”

They took the heavy chain off and the old, worn spiked collar and tossed both into the lake. Sheba watched with great interest.

There was a debate on what to do with Sadie’s body.

Christy said, “Daddy, let’s ask Sheba.”

“Sheba, should we bury Sadie here?” There were three headshakes no.

“Sheba, should we cremate Sadie and keep the ashes in a nice urn?” There were three headshakes yes.

“Christy, I can’t believe what we are seeing! Sheba seems to be as smart as Braveheart. This is very unusual. I have to talk to your Aunt Ashley about this.”

“Daddy, I’m so happy. Thank you so much. I love you! Sheba, you will be my best friend.”

The rest of the SWAT teams reported back that they had picked up a “shell shocked” Slim, stopped the pickup truck and arrested Big Sam. With the video and voice evidence that IQ recorded, they would be going to jail for a very long time. Additional charges of threats of bodily harm to minors would be added.

After Chief Danny debriefed the 5 kids more thoroughly and took the drones, video and voice chips for evidence, the kids got together, discussed the whole event, did some high fives and had a group hug. They vowed to protect each other at all times, just like they did that day. They called themselves, “Team Badass,” and they set up special one button alarms on their phones in case of emergency. They picked a rally spot to meet up with weapons, phones, equipment and their E-Scooters if the alarm ever sounded.

When Christy took Sheba home after her dad called Maria and warned her about the kitty, she expected all Hell to break loose. In fact, her mom was intrigued with Sheba and became friends with her almost immediately, especially after hearing that Sheba seemed to understand English. Maria asked Sheba if she would please not tear up the furniture with her claws, and she would make her a big scratching pad of berber carpet over plywood. Sheba nodded yes three times. Maria hated that some people would declaw their cats and thought it was cruel and unnecessary.

Christy asked Lea to come over and look at the cut on Sheba's shoulder, and Lea patched it up with the latest antibiotic cream, pain killer and a product called "Kwik Heal." She also treated Christy's scraped up knee with similar products. IQ and Ely dropped in to see Sheba and stroke her fur. Even Ben, who was a big dog lover, liked this new addition. Vickie could feel the love given off by this whole family and decided she loved this new assignment. She would be the smartest cat they would ever know.

Sadie was wrapped in a blanket and flown by drone to the vet, where she was cremated and put in a beautiful urn engraved with her name and a figure of a female pitbull. When she was delivered to Danny and Maria's home and put on a shelf in a prominent location, Sheba whined and "meow cried" for a full hour, pacing back and forth and looking up at the urn. Christy talked real sweetly to her, and she finally calmed down.

Danny and Christy made a large scratch pad and a very large sandbox under cover in the backyard. Christy asked Sheba to please use the scratchpad and if she would use the new sandbox. There were three nods yes. They got her a new pretty collar/harness to go for walks. The other kids brought her toys and a special catnip doll which she went nuts over.

She decided to protect this family with her life.

Chapter 9
Stumpy

Ely was at IQ's house for dinner when IQ decided to ask his mom and dad if he could have one of the rescue dogs for a pet. Christy and Sheba had gone for a walk right after dinner, and IQ thought it was the perfect time to ask. He had a convincing speech already prepared, but he didn't need it. When he said, "Daddy, I've never asked you and Mom for anything."

His dad surprised him and said, "Yes IQ, you can have a dog." He knew something was on IQ's mind, and he had been asked several times before about getting a dog when IQ was younger. "We know how very responsible you are."

IQ and Ely started dancing around with joy and hugging both parents. They had never seen him so happy. He and Ely were hugging and kissing each other, and Maria was thinking, "Maybe I need to have 'The Talk' with them soon? They are growing closer and closer."

Ely was getting more beautiful and well built by the day, and she wondered if IQ knew how lucky he was. She was so sweet also, helping out around their house, jumping up to help with the dishes and volunteering for any other chore. Maria knew she didn't want to hang around at her own mother's house. Her mother hated men and the fact that she had a daughter with just a slight deformity. She had told her daughter that guys would just want her for sex, possibly abuse her and would toss her away. Maria had only talked to her mother a couple of times and found her to be somewhat of a cold fish. She was working several jobs to stay afloat. Maria knew that IQ was trying to think of a way to help without offending her or have her think he just wanted her daughter.

After supper Danny went to the Lanai to watch a game on TV, and Maria decided to talk to the kids.

She said, "IQ and Ely, can we have a talk over here on the couch?"

They looked at each other and cracked up with laughter. IQ had told Ely to expect it one day.

"Mom, is this the big 'Sex Talk?' We wondered when it was coming."

"Oh my God!" Maria thought out loud, "This kid is always one step ahead of me!"

Ely had turned beet red, and IQ laughed even more. "Ely, you're blushing!"

Ely looked at Maria and said, "Mama T., I wish you were my real mama!" She went over and hugged Maria with tears running down her face. "My mom won't talk to me about it or tell me anything at all. IQ had to explain everything to me. Don't worry, we would never do anything to ever hurt your trust. We plan to wait until we graduate!"

Maria couldn't believe how sweet this girl was, and to call her Mama T. just made her heart swell. She also felt very relieved.

IQ said, "Mom don't worry. I plan to marry Miss Ely as soon as we graduate, and we won't do anything until then. There is only one problem, Miss Ely. If mom was your real mom, we'd be brother and sister!"

Now they all laughed. IQ said, "Miss Ely, we have to hustle over to the Shelter to look at the dogs. I asked them to stay open late just for us, and we only have an hour."

As they were leaving, Ely turned around and ran back to hug Maria and ran out to the Lanai to hug Danny and called him Papa T. She thanked them both for supper.

Maria went out to the Lanai and Danny said, "Ely called me Papa T., what's that all about?"

"Well, I'm now Mama T., and I think that's going to be our daughter in law in a few years, and I couldn't be happier!"

"I have to agree, and that's one lucky boy. Now come over here for your own hug."

Ely and IQ made it to the shelter with time to spare and got some bad news. Two of the severely deformed puppies had died, but the rest were doing well, especially the biggest one. This dog was like nothing the shelter people had ever seen. It seemed to get bigger overnight and was very alert. If not for the missing left paw, it could walk around normally.

The other puppies were looking for bottled milk, but this one seemed to want real food. IQ and Ely were fascinated and called to it. The pup came right over to them to get petted. He licked their hands and was very friendly. Even IQ couldn't figure out what kind it was.

It looked like part Irish Wolfhound, part German Shepard, part Bernese Mountain dog and a little real Wolf thrown in. He couldn't figure out how Sadie, a pitbull, could have given birth to such an oddball. It was going to be huge. Well, Miss Ely wanted it, and that was good enough for him. He asked the shelter to keep it for them for two more days. That would give them time to pick up bedding, food, etc. Ely was thrilled, but they wondered how Sheba would react when they brought it home.

"Ely, If it's ok with you, we're going to name him Stumpy, and I plan to give him a working paw. My team at Microdots are working on stuff like that as a side line. We can give him a paw with feedback into his leg if things go correctly."

"IQ, that's wonderful!" More hugs and kisses came his way!

Ely and IQ got the very best dog food, a huge bed, toys, a custom collar and a strong leash. When they went back to the shelter in two days, they found an astounded staff member who told them that the dog seemed to be some kind of freak of nature. It was eating everything they could give it and had almost doubled in size again. Even IQ couldn't believe it, though he did have a premonition about this dog during the rescue. They were sad to hear that another of Sadie's puppies had died despite all the efforts to save it.

Jim in Level 2 was especially distraught that 3 of his babies had died. The one with the missing ear was doing well, as was the one with the missing tail. The one with the bulging eyes was being treated by an expert who IQ had brought in, and it was expected to be ok. The staff was sure they would all be adopted.

"Jim, this is where you go back for part two, your last assignment."

"Ok Bill, what's the job? I still feel bad about Sadie and 3 of my puppies though."

"Jim, you did the best you could, and I got word that you will be taking over for me after this last assignment. So give it your best shot."

"Bill, that's great news, thank you!"

Suddenly, Jim found himself in Stumpy and heard IQ and Miss Ely calling to him. He found it hard to walk and did a kind of skip walk over to them. My God, he could feel the love coming off of those two, and Miss Ely smelled like a fresh bouquet of flowers, just delightful. He was thinking everything was going to be fine.

"Hello Stumpy. Come here, big guy. We're going to take you home. Nobody will try to hurt you again. Would you like that?"

Jim decided to nod three times, just like he was told Chewie and Braveheart used to do. He decided to be a genius dog and have some fun with them.

IQ said, "Ely, did you see that? You don't suppose it's possible for Stumpy to be like Sheba? Supposedly Chewie and Braveheart used to do that exact same thing."

"IQ, it's almost too much of a coincidence. Something else is going on here. Let's ask Stumpy some more questions when we get him to your place."

IQ called for one of his special Microdots' drones to pick them up. It's the only type of drone he trusted to fly in. It had his patented parachute safety system in case of total electronic system failure, and he made sure his whole family and Miss Ely always flew in one of them. He was raking in millions of dollars just on his passenger drone sales business alone. He made even more cash retro-fitting other companies' drones with his parachute system. Stumpy laid across Ely's lap and napped for the short trip while she smiled at IQ and petted Stumpy. Arriving at his Mom and Dad's house, they decided to cautiously introduce Stumpy to Sheba. This could go badly if things went sideways.

"Oh my God, is that you Vickie?"

"You have got to be kidding me! Jim, is that you inside of that dog with the bum leg that Sadie had? You got really big in just a few days."

"Yep, it's me, and I'm hungry all the time. I don't know how bloody big I'll get, but God am I happy to see you! They named me Stumpy."

"Well, how appropriate is that! Come here big guy."

Sheba walked right over to Stumpy and rubbed against him, and he gave her a lick. They started to play together, and Sheba showed Stumpy her favorite toy, the catnip doll. He was intrigued by it and said, "Wow, this is great, they must really love you!"

Vickie said, "Yes, especially Christy, but the whole family is just great, and I can tell how much that Ely girl loves you just by watching her expressions."

"Yes, and we are supposed to protect them all, especially all the kids."

"Sounds pretty easy to me Jim, if we team up."

"For sure Vickie, and we can have a little fun showing them how smart we are."

IQ, Ely, Christy, and Maria were astounded by how well the two pets got along. It seemed like they almost knew each other.

They decided to ask Stumpy a couple of questions.

IQ asked Stumpy if he remembered Sheba from the cabin after just being born, never expecting an answer. Stumpy gave three yes nods. Then he asked Stumpy if he remembered his mother Sadie after he was born, and he nodded yes three more times and started to whine almost like crying. They all were amazed, and Stumpy went over to Ely with tears in his big brown eyes.

She picked him up, and he put his head on her shoulder still making whining noises.

Ely stroked him and told him everything would be OK now. They would take good care of him. "Let's not ask him any more questions right now, IQ." It's the first time that IQ ever saw Ely frown at him, and he apologized profusely.

"Ely, I'm so sorry. I never expected him to remember that. It was a dumb thing for me to do."

Vickie said, "Aw Jim, I'm sorry I couldn't save your Mom. I just couldn't get out of that cage in time."

"Vickie, it's OK. I don't know why I'm feeling so bad. I should be glad this family has me."

"Come on and we'll play with some of the cool toys, and maybe they will feed us soon."

"OK Vickie."

Stumpy wiggled to get down and seemed ready to play with Sheba, so Ely put him down near her. All seemed well again, and they got along famously.

It was late afternoon and getting towards suppertime, and they decided to feed both Stumpy and Sheba at the same time. Stumpy chowed down in typical dog fashion, while Sheba ate more demurely, although quite a bit. This was going to be a costly pair to feed, but Maria's business was doing extremely well and IQ was loaded, so no problems there.

Chapter 10
Future MIL Problem?

Ely received a rare call from her mom while everyone was watching the pets eat.

She looked a little distressed, and IQ asked if everything was OK at home.

"Mom thinks I'm spending too much time over here and not doing enough chores at home, but I do all kinds of chores. I think she's a little jealous."

"Miss Ely, I think it's time I met your mom. I can't believe we haven't met after all these months."

Ely pulled him aside and said, "I don't know IQ, she thinks you are just trying to get in my panties, as she put it." Ely turned red and could barely look at IQ, but saw he had a wide smile on his face.

"Your mom is just being protective given all the past history with your dad and some other poor male choices she made. Maybe I can change her mind. It's worth a try."

"Well OK, but she wants me to cook something, and she's having trouble with the AC as well."

"Miss Ely, I can solve both those problems in a 'Florida heartbeat,' as Grandpa BD always says."

IQ called for his private drone and asked his main man Harold, AKA, "The Hulk," to load a tool kit in it with special AC parts. The fancy drone showed up in minutes with a large lighted M on both sides signifying the Microdots company. IQ asked Ely what her Mom's favorite meal was and she told him the eggplant parmesan from Ricardo's. IQ called for a large order for four people to be delivered about 15 minutes after their arrival at Ely's home. With the plush drone doing all the work, IQ apologized to Ely again for asking such a stupid question to Stumpy. He never thought the dog would actually understand English as well as he did. He wondered how in the whole wide world could their family end up with two more genius type pets. It was very suspicious, especially after the Chewie and Braveheart dogs.

It turned out that Miss Ely was not mad at him and smothered him in kisses all the way to her Mom's house. All that time he was thinking and dreaming about the panties remark and how they could possibly keep their promise to wait. The drone landed with just enough room on the driveway to spare, and Ely's mom came out to see what the commotion was all about. To say she was impressed would be an understatement. Her mouth hung open as IQ jumped out and pushed the button to automatically open Ely's side. He gave Ely a hand to get down just for show.

IQ had put on a cap with Microdots stitched on it, and he quickly removed it, stuck out his hand and said, "Good evening Mrs. Simmons, I'm Dean Benjamin Turner, but everyone calls me IQ. I'm so sorry that we haven't met sooner, but with work at my Microdots Company, school, doing chores at home and helping Miss Ely with her homework, I'm pretty well whipped by the end of the day. Really though, that's no excuse for not meeting Miss Ely's mom. She mentions you often."

Ely's mom was for once, almost speechless. She was prepared for some uncouth school kid who wanted her pretty daughter for only one thing, but she found an actual young, well dressed gentleman smiling at her.

She took his extended hand for a quick shake and said hello.

IQ said, "Mrs. Simmons, Ely said you had a problem with your AC, so would it be ok if I took a look at it. I'm quite the electronics expert, and I brought along a set of tools. May I ask if there was a lightning strike anywhere near this area recently?"

She said there was one fairly close the night before, and that was when the trouble started.

IQ said it was probably something simple like the capacitor which started the fan and compressor outside. He asked if he could go out back and check it out. She said yes, but the AC company wanted hundreds of dollars just to come and check it out, and she didn't have that amount. IQ told her that his beautiful, best friend's Mom would never be charged for anything like that. He told her that he had ordered supper for all of them, and asked Miss Ely to set the table as the drone should arrive in 10 or 15 minutes. Once again, Mrs. Simmons was speechless.

Ely was smiling to herself, this was IQ at his charming best. She said, "Mom, IQ asked what your favorite meal was and ordered it from Ricardo's. Isn't he a sweetheart? And no, he doesn't want anything from me in return. He is my very best friend ever!"

IQ was correct, the capacitor was shot, and he had guessed correctly on the model and brand after quizzing Ely. He had it changed in 8 minutes flat. AC back on and hands washed, he finished up just as the food drone landed. "I'll get the order Mrs. Simmons. Ely, can you help me carry in everything?"

Outside at the delivery drone, IQ tacked on a generous tip to the computer screen.

Ely smiled at him and said, "IQ, I love you so much. I bet you could charm a snake."

They put the food on the table, and IQ held the chair for Ely's mom, much to her surprise. IQ didn't care much for the delicious eggplant parmesan, but crammed some down anyhow. There were garlic rolls, angel hair pasta and broccoli, all Mrs. Simmon's favorites. He told her that he guessed on dessert and got strawberry cheesecake. She commented that he got way too much, but he said she could have leftovers and that he had ordered extra sauce if needed. She couldn't believe her luck and started to really like this kid. Ely had done alright for herself.

During the meal and evening, IQ commented on the great choice of names for Ely, hers being Eva, and the fact that she had blue eyes as pretty as Miss Ely's. IQ told her how intelligent Ely was and that she was now ranked 5th in their class of 155 students in the Charter School, no small feat. He mentioned that intelligence usually is inherited from the mother and asked where she worked. He said that Ely told him she worked way too hard to provide for them. He found out that one of her main jobs was as a receptionist at a tightwad company he knew of. IQ offered her a job at twice the amount she was making with full benefits including healthcare. His oldest employee was retiring soon, so it would be a perfect fit. She would have to be polite, but shrewd, as they produced very sensitive equipment for the government that many unscrupulous people would like to know about.

Eva choked up and was getting teary eyed as she thanked IQ for everything. He said, "Nothing is too good for my Ely or her family." He told her he would send a Microsoft drone to pick her up on Monday at 7:45 AM sharp and to quit her other job. IQ actually got a hug from Eva, and Ely walked him out to the M-Drone.

She whispered, "IQ, you may see those panties sooner than you imagined."

They wanted to really do a deep kiss, but her mom was watching, and they settled on a cheek kiss and hug instead.

Eva commented to Ely, "Young Lady, you did really well on that pick of men. He's wonderful."

Ely relied, "Oh Mom, I know, I absolutely adore him. He is so kind to me. If anything bad ever happened to him, I don't know what I'd do." Poor Ely didn't know what was coming!

On the short trip back to his house, all IQ could think about were those panties. It was driving him crazy. He had seen how great she looked in a bikini, so why would the panty comment drive him nuts? How in the world could they ever wait another 4-½ years until graduation?

Chapter 11
The Master Plan

Wallace Schmidt and Cory Hills had been planning their kidnapping operation for many months. They were in the last stages now and were growing very impatient, but they knew they couldn't afford to make even one mistake. That IQ kid was too well known with the top cop for a father and government connections through his Microdots Company. They had purchased several burner phones and a second van, this one being a beat up green one with fake tree service signs on the sides. Inside on both they had installed several eyebolts and stashed duct tape and rope. Cory had purchased a very old, J-frame Smith and Wesson .38 caliber revolver from another felon friend who assured him it worked. It only held 5 rounds and was a short barreled, double action only gun making it a little more inaccurate. Convicted felons could not legally purchase guns or ammo, so they would have to make do without test firing. They stashed that in the van also, as they weren't allowed to be caught carrying a weapon.

Their biggest stroke of luck came when they read the article about the deserted cabin on the lake where the dog fighting ring guys had squatted. Odd that the very kid they were going to kidnap was instrumental in their capture. It took them quite a while to locate the cabin and find the best route to and from it by van. It was still hidden and even more overgrown. They cleaned it up inside as best they could, but they left the crime scene tape and no trespassing signs as they were. Their next problem was figuring out how to pull off the kidnapping, how to get the ransom delivered without being tracked and how to get away without being caught. They decided to have Cory's friend, Max, drive the white van away in the opposite direction after transferring the kid to the green van. The green van would be stashed a couple of miles away from the kidnapping area. If he was stopped on the main roads, he would act innocent and say he just bought it very cheap from a couple of guys to make a few bucks doing some yard work. Unknown to Cory's friend, they planned to make a quick call with one of the burner phones saying they saw a suspicious guy in a white van who had a kid inside. Then they would destroy the phone or shut it off and throw it into the lake. That should confuse the cops for quite a while.

They scouted the very big lake with the old rowboat for hours looking for a getaway boat, and they finally came upon a closed up snowbird house with an EV type airboat on a trailer beside the house. Ringing the bell casually brought no results, and they had planned to ask for directions if someone answered. They were able to push the trailer and airboat by hand to the water and cut the tie downs loose. They floated the airboat and pushed the trailer deeper into the water, letting it sink. It would appear to any neighbors that the house owners had decided to take the airboat up north with them. The airboat was an old EV style, but it held its charge well. They did this in the evening and slowly cruised back to the cabin making as little noise as possible. They knew the airboat could do 60 knots fairly quietly, not like the extremely loud old ICE models. This would be their third getaway vehicle, and they planned to glide up the shallow area next to the snowbird house and steal his garaged second car to make a clean getaway with the loot.

The most difficult parts of the plan would be the actual kidnapping and the ransom transfer. There were many ways to track a ransom since most transactions were now electronic. They planned to ask for $5 million in actual cash, not a huge amount in the 2080's economy, and it would probably be easy for the parents and/or the kid's company to come up with. They would have it delivered to an open area under high tension power lines where another generic untrackable drone would latch on and deliver it to them. It would take a drone able to lift a sizable amount of weight, as $5 million in fifties and hundreds would be quite a load. This they got from a stolen batch of drones that another friend of Cory's had heisted from a delivery truck. They got two more identical drones to create a diversion when the ransom was delivered.

They decided to do the kidnapping on a Sunday morning when the kid, his girlfriend and a gigantic mutt would always take a leisurely walk. The "Heinz 57" looking mutt could present a problem, but it looked slow and dopey to them. They would take a big club along to neutralize it if they had to. Very few people were out and about at that time of day, but they had to check for cops who always seemed to be tailing those kids. They had a plan to get the cops away long enough for the kidnapping to take place. They would start a small fire in an abandoned building, a dumpster or even a snowbird's house if necessary, then call it in as they were driving back to grab the kid. They would ditch the burner phone on the way back. Cory and Wallace went over the plan many times and only had to pick a Sunday.

Chapter 12
Microdots Company

IQ's company was growing so fast that a major expansion was in process led by two of his most prized employees, Harold Adams, nicknamed "The Hulk" by the other employees and Olive Oles, nicknamed "Olive Oil." IQ instructed his employees to call them by their proper names if they valued their jobs, but occasional jokes persisted in private. The employees loved IQ and their jobs and couldn't see ever working anywhere else. He paid extremely well, they had great benefits and he had monthly parties with food and entertainment. There was an onsite cafeteria, lounge and workout room with showers. They all knew enough not to abuse the privileges and would not let him down.

The new large building had a class III section which housed all of the top secret government projects. There was one project in process so extremely sensitive in nature that only Olive, Harold and IQ knew about it or were permitted to enter the room. There was a 3 way authentication process required just to enter the room, by card, eye scan and facial recognition, which couldn't be defeated. All three people had to enter within 45 seconds or the room would be locked down. The manufacturing process was so secret that none of the other employees even knew what the latest gadget was used for. It was on a need to know only basis. IQ, Harold, and Olive had many conversations about how the new gadget could be seriously misused if it fell into the wrong hands. IQ brought his dad, Chief Danny Turner, in to discuss it, and he provided some valuable insight about how to control those who may have plans to misuse it or even sell the gadget or idea to the wrong people. IQ knew this could make him a multi-billionaire, and he would handsomely reward his workers if all went according to plan. He particularly trusted Olive and Harold and frequently told them so. He had to chuckle to himself sometimes, as they were the typical Jack Spratt couple. Harold was a big, wide, solid guy with a big head, and Olive was very tall and slender. They both were really fond of each other and told IQ so separately, but he thought it best if they worked it out by themselves. They would bring each other special treats or coffee, but they were both too shy to get anything serious going. Maybe Ely could think of a plan to get them together. They were only 25 and 26 years old, but time waits for no one.

As promised, a drone showed up for Ely's Mom and whisked her to work in no time.

Eva stared out the windows in amazement on the short trip, and then she saw IQ walk out to greet her. He held his arm out to help her down and greeted her warmly. He asked if he could call her Eva as he introduced her around the office. Everyone was so welcoming and warm that she almost cried. This was the direct opposite of all her previous jobs. Jane, the lady set to retire, was introduced and took her to where she would work. She had the employment forms already filled out to sign. She emphasized the extremely sensitive nature of some of the products and how to spot phony or nefarious people trying to get in, obtain information or wrangle a tour. Eva was a quick learner and could be tough if necessary. Everyone raved about working there and about how kind IQ was, so she knew he wasn't faking anything. He was the real deal, and she would do her absolute best. Ely showed up and handed her two cards, one for an exclusive clothing store and one for the top hairdresser in town. She said IQ wanted her to look sharp in her new role, but thought she already looked great, just like her daughter. This time she did break down and cry a little and told Ely to never break that boy's heart.

Things went so much better for Ely at home after that, and the whole Turner gang could tell the difference. Ely was even more happy and loving than usual and a delight to have around. She just loved the big family, especially the "Team BadAss" gang, but thought maybe IQ was working way too hard, as he looked a little tense at times.

Chapter 13
K-9 Meet and Greet

Stumpy was growing bigger by the day and was now much heavier than a full grown male German Shepherd. IQ wanted to fit him for a new left paw, but wasn't sure what size he was going to be. But then he thought, "What the heck, we can fit him with a new one every month and leave the electrodes connected in the leg." Stumpy loved his new paw and could finally walk pretty well. He loved IQ, Ely and especially Sheba, his best friend. Ben asked Stumpy one day if he would like to meet the three department K-9 dogs, and he nodded yes three times.

Christy asked what would happen if they took Sheba along. They decided on a careful test run, and Ben asked Sheba if she would like to meet the K-9 dogs. There were another three nods yes. IQ and Ely were both busy, so Ben and Christy took the two pets along to the early morning briefing. The three K-9 dogs consisted of two Belgian Malinois, Saber and Lance, and a German Shepherd named Chopper. The two Belgians were about 80 pounds each, and Chopper was about 105 pounds.

Bill up in Level 2 was observing all this with a little concern, especially the plan to introduce Sheba to the K-9s. He contacted Jim and said, "I'm going to give you and Vickie a little of the old 'Jedi Mind Tricks' from those ancient Star Wars movies. You can both use them to make quick friends with those tough K-9s."

"Well, Ok Bill, we'll give them a try."

Ben had a leash on Stumpy who now weighed over 165 pounds and still loved to eat. He was not fat though, and the Vet said he was in perfect condition except for that left paw. IQ had the latest model on him, and he could walk pretty well with just a slight limp.

Christy also had Sheba on a leash, and she looked her normal gorgeous, slinky self.

Both Ben and Christy had their intern uniforms on when they entered 30 minutes early to attend the morning briefing.. They thought possibly the K-9s could be carefully introduced to Sheba and Stumpy. The K-9 officers were a little skeptical, but they had heard how intelligent those two were, even perfectly understanding English and able to answer every question. They wanted to put them to the test and prove or disprove the rumors. Every officer liked both Ben and Christy and thought they were quick learners who would make great cops someday. After commenting on Stumpy's size and marveling at how big Sheba was for a supposedly normal cat, they cautiously brought out the K-9s. Well, to their amazement, all the animals greeted each other like long time friends due to the little mind control tricks from Stumpy and Sheba. The K-9s acted like Stumpy and Sheba were king and queen of the precinct. After a few minutes Stumpy had the K-9s sitting in a row with He and Sheba opposite them. It looked like an animal briefing, and the officers were staring like they couldn't believe their eyes. Actually Jim and Vickie were telling the K-9s that they might need their help someday to protect their family and to be alert.

Suddenly the door opened, and the three countywide Chief, Josh Wilder, arrived in a surprise visit. Sumter County Chief, Danny Turner, came out to greet him and yelled "Attention" to his officers. Everyone formed up including the K-9s, with Stumpy and Sheba turning around and sitting down in front of them. Chief Wilder saluted the officers, and when he glanced over at the K-9s, he saw a massive dog and a large cat saluting him.

"What in the world do we have here? Are these the two I've been hearing about?"

He saw Christy and Ben, his favorite interns, standing at attention and told everyone, "At Ease. How in the heck did you teach these two to do that, especially the big cat? I hear they are very difficult to train."

"Sir, the odd thing is, we didn't teach them that. They must have picked it up from watching. They are very intelligent."

"Vickie, is this fun, or what?"

"Jim, you were right, maybe we can show them some more tricks."

"Chief Wilder, why don't you ask them some questions? That will prove that they can understand English," said Christy.

"OK, I'll do just that. Stumpy, can you show me where Chopper is?"

Stumpy nodded three times and walked over, sat down beside Chopper and put his leg and paw around him.

"Amazing! Sheba, can you please show us where the framed knife collection is?"

Sheba nodded three times, looked around the large briefing room and walked over to the wall hung knives. She looked up, stood on her hind legs and meowed loudly.

"This is just astounding! I'll be convinced if you both can sit beside Chief Turner."

"Too easy peasy Vickie."

"For sure Jim. I wonder if Chief Turner has any treats in his office? After all, you haven't eaten in about an hour," she said, laughing.

"Sure, torture me Vickie."

They both were laughing as they walked over and sat by Chief Turner, one on each side.

"That is the most incredible thing I've seen or heard about since the stories that were told of Chewie and Braveheart. Let's talk in your office Chief Turner. Maybe we could use those two as spies sometime. They could work as our CIs'."

Jim and Vickie followed them in to see if the Chief, indeed, had any treats. It turned out that he did have a box of chews that he occasionally gave to the K-9s. Stumpy sniffed them out and begged a little bit. Danny got out two snacks, but Stumpy went to the office window and gave a little bark.

Danny thought he knew what he wanted and said, "Oh, you want some for your new friends. Here are three more."

Stumpy and Sheba grabbed the 5 snacks and headed out the door and over to where the K-9s were getting ready to go out on patrol. They dropped a treat in front of each dog.

The well trained dogs looked at their handlers to get permission to eat and got the OK. All five downed the treats. Even Vickie liked hers because it was a meaty type, not one of those dry dog treats. From then on the 3 K-9s were good friends. Stumpy watched the handlers get the dogs ready to go out on patrol. The handlers in the past usually put the old style heavy bulletproof vests on them, but the officers now used the very lightweight and almost invisible coverings invented by IQ's company called "Invisa-shield." It cost IQ a good deal of money to develop and produce these, and the market was small in comparison to his other products. But IQ had a soft spot for animals and children and would always do what he could to protect and help them. When he first demonstrated the "Invisa-shield," there was great skepticism, but he demonstrated its capability by covering a large dog sized block of ballistic gel and firing service weapons into it from all angles. Run by miniature batteries, the "Invisa-shield" would instantly spread the shock out around the entire block of gel instead of concentrating it in one area. It worked so well that he patented it for human vests also.

The vests were much more comfortable to wear and proved themselves many times in many situations. The military started to order large quantities, and now IQ was making great profits on both types. The only problems occurred when the users failed to do a battery check before heading out on patrol. IQ included multiple and large warning labels on every order. The rechargeable batteries in the units would also cause the vests to alert when they were down to 25%. Stumpy and Sheba hung around until lunchtime when Ben and Christy took them home and regaled Maria with the day's adventures. They got even more treats and love when they got home.

Chapter 14
Almost A Disaster Day

It was a beautiful Sunday morning, and Ely and IQ decided to go on their normal slow walk with Stumpy. They asked Christy if she and Sheba would like to go along, but Sheba was napping across Christy's lap, and she told them she would take her out later.

As they were getting ready to walk, Bill from up in Level 2 chimed in and said, "Jim, trouble is coming, put on the Invis-Shield."

"OK Bill, I'll see if I can get IQ to put it on me."

"Get stubborn Jim, Stumpy will need this!"

As Ely got the leash ready, Stumpy walked over to the closet where the Invisa-Shield was kept and barked.

Ely said, "IQ, Stumpy wants something in the closet."

IQ knew that there were only human jackets and the vest and asked Stumpy, "Do you want to try the 'Invisa-Shield' vest on for size?"

Stumpy nodded three times for yes.

IQ checked the battery, and it was at 95%. IQ thought it was odd, but anything that Stumpy wanted was OK with him. You could barely see it on Stumpy, and he seemed pleased, so why not. Ely gave him one of her sweet smiles, and all was right with the world. "God, I love that girl so much! Please protect her always."

They headed out and turned down the exact street that Wallace, Cory and Max, who was driving, were waiting in the white van. As they started down the block everything looked deserted, so the gang decided to do the kidnapping. The threesome quickly drove around the block and about a half mile to an old building where they started a fire to draw the cops away from their assigned protection detail. The fire was quickly set, and Wallace called it in, saying people were in danger and the exact location. They threw the cell phone onto a passing landscaping trailer going in the opposite direction and hightailed it back to the block where the kids were walking. The kids were almost to the end of the block when the white van came to a screeching stop. IQ was suspicious and thought something odd was happening. When Wallace and Cory jumped out, he told Ely to run home and call Dad as soon as possible. Ely hesitated and almost got caught by big Wallace. She took off running, and Wallace knew he had no chance of catching her. Cory was disappointed, as he wanted that hot blonde for himself, but he had to hold on to IQ.

IQ shouted at Ely, "Use the locket, use the locket," but got slammed in the temple with Cory's gun, knocking him out and breaking his glasses.

Stumpy was slow to react, but he finally barked and started to attack Cory. As he started towards Cory, he got slammed in the head with the club by Wallace and knocked out. Ely had been looking over her shoulder while sprinting for IQ's house and saw what happened to IQ and Stumpy. She almost stopped and was thinking of running back to help when she saw IQ and Stumpy thrown into the white van.

"The locket, how do I use the locket? Help me God! What did IQ tell me about the locket two years ago?" As she neared the house she remembered. Press twice, then hold the button down. But she couldn't remember how long, so she just continued to hold her finger on it, and all Hell broke loose.

Every phone in the family, the police headquarters, all Microdots Co. employees, and the FBI and CIA hotlines started blaring a special ringtone. Something was going down, and it wasn't good. Maria, working at her desk, was startled by the ringing and looked at her outside cameras on her big screen. She saw Ely with tears flowing from her eyes running towards the house and knew something bad must have happened. She rushed to the front door and pulled Ely in, quickly locking the door. Christy and Sheba, who were both napping, woke up with a start and asked what was happening. Ely was almost hysterical and could barely speak. She finally gasped out that IQ and Stumpy were hurt by two guys and kidnapped. Christy grabbed her phone and pushed the "Team Badass" button. Ben, Lea, IQ and Elys' phones all blared out the emergency signal. Ben and Lea quickly left their house and headed toward the meeting spot with all their gear. Sheba was in a panic and tried to contact Stumpy, but she got no response. IQ's phone was taken, smashed and thrown out the white van's window, but it still emitted a location signal.

Sheba was saying, "Jim, Jim, Stumpy, Stumpy, please talk to me!"

Vickie got no answer, so she tried Bill, up in Level 2.

"Bill, help me, where is Jim? Is he OK? Please help!" There was no answer.

Christy was listening to Ely describe the white van and the two men, or possibly three, as someone else appeared to be driving. She told her Mom that she had to take Sheba outside to the sandbox and would be right back in. Instead, she snuck into her Dad's "Man Cave" first, then went outside with Sheba and disappeared. She jumped on her E-Scooter and headed for the secret meeting spot with Sheba wrapped around her shoulder hanging on tightly.

Chief Danny contacted Maria almost immediately after getting the emergency ringtone. After getting all the information, he immediately contacted every officer he had and put them on special 24 hour duty. No vacations, no special leaves, not even a sick day until his son and Stumpy were found. The FBI and CIA were both informed, and immediately many teams were sent out toward that location, as IQ was designated as a "National Security Priority1" person due to his sensitive work with them. Satellite images were scanned for information and redirected to show the Villages. It was a huge task since The Villages now had a population of at least 500,000. Danny was extremely worried about his son. He knew how badly these things could go if not handled correctly. He radioed the two-man detail who were supposed to be watching IQ, Ely and Stumpy on their walk and read them the riot act. He ripped them up, down and sideways and told them to find his son. He told them that they had one damn assignment, and they blew it. He calmed down a little after they explained that they had seen no one in the area and responded to a close-by fire call with possible casualties. The kids were attacked on a side street they hadn't used before and that they had rushed back immediately after finding out the fire was a diversion.

At Microdots, IQ's right hand man, Harold, who had been working a little overtime that Sunday, was startled by the claxon blasting throughout the facility, but quickly remembered the protocol. All hands on deck, building locked down, Priority 3, everybody must report for duty. Harold sent a special passenger drone for Eva, since she would be worried about Ely. He sent one for Olive, just because she was special to him. It took almost an hour, but when everyone was assembled, he told them what had happened and that nobody leaves until IQ is found. He gave the word to launch the search drones and to cover one square mile with each drone in a grid pattern searching for a white van or any suspicious vehicle. Many of the team were in a panic, since IQ was the only man who would give them a chance to work and not question their background, their looks or any deformities. They would work their butts off for him. Microdots' drones went up in all directions with a lighted M on the bottom, and many photos were taken of them by viewers on the ground. There were so many that it looked like bats pouring out of a cave. There were hundreds of drones scanning the whole area, and Harold and Olive used AI to look through the huge amount of data coming in. No white vans were found.

Harold checked the employees list and found that only one employee was missing. It was 65 year old Albert Johnson, a down and out black veteran, who had asked IQ for a job one day outside of the Microdots building. IQ asked him what was good at, and Albert told him he was a good janitor, but no one would hire him because of his age. IQ hired him on the spot, but told him he had to be very good at his job because of the specifications required with many of the extremely tiny and sensitive products they produced. Albert was very good at his job and had already gotten a couple of raises. He told everyone that he would walk through fire for IQ and that IQ had saved him from losing his small home. Harold decided to call him, and he found out that he was out sick with yet another strain of Covid, but improving daily. He had notified the office about it. He told Harold he would immediately send up his own personal small drone given to him by IQ, since his house was on the outskirts of the Villages and out of the grid search area.

Eva arrived via the roof entrance guarded by the security team, since all other entrances to the office and factory had barricades that immediately deployed when the claxon sounded. All windows had bulletproof glass with clear hurricane shutters that rolled down when the alarm went off. She was terribly worried about Ely and especially IQ. He had restored her faith in men and treated Ely and herself like they were the most special ladies in the world. She didn't pray much, but now she sent up constant prayers for IQ's safe return. She made a quick call to Maria and thanked her profusely for taking care of Ely. She talked quickly to Ely telling her she loved her. She went immediately to her desk and started fielding hundreds of calls without giving out too much information. The press had gotten wind of something big going down, but they were told very little, only that there was an extreme emergency.

Chief Danny called Maria again and told her to do a full lockdown of their house. That meant no one was to come in or go out, and double security doors and windows would activate when she pressed the code in.

Maria was in a panic and said, "Danny, Christy went out with Sheba to the sandbox, but they didn't come back to the main house. I checked all the cameras and didn't see her anywhere."

"Maria, check the recording of the back of the house on your computer."

"Danny, I see her getting out her E-Scooter and taking off with Sheba hanging on to her back. She has something in a small shoulder bag."

Some bad thoughts were popping into Danny's head. Those darn kids were planning to search for IQ. Suddenly, he thought of something that Christy might do, but he hoped she wouldn't.

"Maria, go into the 'Man Cave' and see if anything looks out of place."

"Danny, there is something odd. There is that book shelf that looks like it dropped open on the bottom. There is a foam liner with holes cut in it. There is one that looks like a gun shape and two other empty rectangular slots. Your desk drawer is open and a white card is laying on top."

"Oh Hell Maria, that shelf is called a 'tactical trap' to hide guns and magazines. It had Poppop's old Colt M1911A1 .45 caliber from his time in the Korean War and two fully loaded magazines. Christy must have known where I keep the card that opens the shelf. Check the other top drawer. I hid that huge switchblade in the right hand one."

"It's partially open and empty Danny. You don't suppose those kids are planning some kind of rescue mission, do you?"

"That's exactly what I think. Find out if the other two kids are missing. Keep Ely inside and lockdown the house now. She has seen the kidnappers, and we have to keep her safe."

"Ok Danny. There is a call coming in now from Ashley." After a few seconds of panicked talking, Maria told Danny that Lea and Ben were missing and weren't answering their phones. Both E-Scooters were gone as well as two of the new "Invisa-Shield" vests, Lea's First Aid and Trauma kit and the latest high powered combination shock and bang stick.

"Oh Damn! Keep trying to call the three of them and have them come back. It's too dangerous. Text them also. Please ask Ely if she knows anything about it, but be nice, she might be traumatized. I'll call Andy and give him the bad news. Tell Ashley to lock down her house immediately."

"Ok Danny."

Maria went back into the great room and found Ely kneeling down by the sofa and praying with tears streaming down her face.

Maria heard her saying over and over, "Please God, don't let them hurt IQ anymore and bring him back to us! God, he saved my life! You have to save him!"

Maria said, "Come here sweetheart and sit with me. Papa will find him. He has hundreds of officers out searching. Can you tell me if you know anything about Christy, Lea and Ben going missing?"

"Mama, that second alarm type phone call was for our 'Team Badass' group to meet up at our secret location with the E-Scooters and all our gear. I wish I could have gone along. We just have to find IQ, we just have to!"

Maria knew the kids were long gone from the meeting spot and were on the way to who knows where.

"Ely, I overheard you praying, and you said IQ saved your life. What did you mean by that?"

"Mama, promise you won't get mad at me."

"Oh honey, I won't. You know you can tell me anything."

"Mama, when I first transferred to school, I didn't know anybody. I was picked on and bullied at school and online constantly, just for being different. They would make fun of my hand and even said if they were me, they would kill themselves. I was so sad. I would go home and cry myself to sleep every night. I stole one of Mom's sleeping pills every so often until I had saved a handful. The very day that IQ came over to my table at lunchtime, I was sitting all alone as usual and feeling awful. I planned to take that handful of pills that night and just go to sleep. I would pray that God would forgive me. But instead, He sent me an angel called IQ. He said, 'Miss Ely, would you mind if I sit with you.' He had the sweetest smile and was so kind that I almost cried right there. We talked the entire lunch period, and he offered to get me up to speed on my studies. He said we could study at his house, and he walked to your house with me. Sometimes he would talk in different languages, and he taught me all kinds of things. Then I met you and Papa, and you were both so nice to me. That night

I flushed the pills down the toilet. I love IQ so much. I will never break his heart! We just have to find him, Mama."

Maria was almost in tears as she hugged Ely tightly. "We all love you Ely. You can always tell me anything, and I will never judge you. Please don't ever consider hurting yourself again. I have to call your Aunt Ashley and make sure she is locked down. She's all alone in her house. See if you can get ahold of those three missing members of your gang."

"Yes Mama, I will try." Ely texted and called, but got back only thumbs up texts from them. "Well, at least they are ok," she thought.

Chapter 15
The Kidnappers Plan

Wallace and Cory were congratulating themselves on how great the first part of the plan was working. They had IQ tied up in the white van. The side of his head had bled quite a bit where the glasses had broken, but he was coming around from that hit with the .38. They considered leaving the massive, goofy looking dog, but they dumped him in the van also. They figured they could sell him for a good price if they could locate another dog fighting ring buyer. That mutt must weigh nearly 200 pounds. He was starting to wake up after his hit with Wallace's club. Stumpy opened his eyes and found out he was tied to an eye hook with a short heavy rope. He wanted to rip those guys' throats out. He looked over at IQ and saw blood on his face and cheek, but he was awake and looking around. IQ knew that they had grabbed him for a ransom, and he decided to try and reason with them.

He said, "Guys, if you wanted money, all you had to do was ask. I would have given you lots of cash. It's not too late. We can still make a deal."

Wallace said, "Shut up kid, we have a foolproof plan."

IQ knew that there was no point in arguing with them. He was worrying about Ely and hoping she made it to his house safely.

The white van was exchanged for the green one, and Stumpy and IQ were transferred into it. They had to threaten Stumpy with the gun and the club to get him into the van with IQ. Stumpy knew not to fight. He would pick the time and place to attack. He had to save IQ. Cory's friend took off with the white van in the opposite direction as planned. As soon as he left, Cory turned on a burner phone and called the police. He told them he saw a suspicious white van with a kid inside and maybe a large dog. He gave them the direction it was traveling and quickly shut off the phone. He threw it into a retention pond as they were driving. By this time, they were out of all of the drones' search areas and just by pure luck they weren't spotted.

Max was already miles from the van transfer area when suddenly he was surrounded by police vehicles. He also saw a pure black, huge drone hovering above the road. It was outfitted with rockets and laser tubes all pointing at him. Cops poured out of the EV vans with guns drawn. He decided to try the agreed upon bluff, that he had just bought the van from a couple of guys for a cheap price. The first guy to reach the van happened to be Chief Danny Turner, and he yanked Max out by his shirt, slamming him to the ground. He quickly checked the van out and found it empty. He saw drops of blood on the floor and was outraged.

They had hurt his boy. He grabbed the now handcuffed driver and shoved his 9 MM into his face saying, "Where's my boy, you son of a bitch? I swear to God, I'll put one in your head right now!"

The driver had turned white and tried his excuse. "But Sir, I just bought this van from two guys really cheap a few miles back." He was really scared that the officer was going to pull the trigger. This guy was furious, and his finger was tightening on the trigger. By that time the FBI had gotten to them out of the black drone and cooler heads prevailed.

"Chief Turner, let us interrogate him. We have methods and will immediately inform you." Danny reluctantly backed off, but warned the guy he would find him if anything happened to his son.

It only took about 10 minutes with the FBI until the guy squealed like a pig. He told them about the green van exchange and about being the driver for the kidnapping. He said the boy and some huge dog were OK, but both had been hit by the ringleader, Wallace and by Cory. Danny was still red in the face and knew his blood pressure must be really high, but he was somewhat relieved. The driver swore he didn't know where they were headed, but at least now they were looking for a green van. Danny called Microdots and informed them of the van color change. The previously scanned and recorded info was quickly searched, but no green van turned up. All the drones were recalled for quick recharges and would be sent up again closer to the van exchange area.

Back at the kidnapping scene CSI people had found drops of blood, a smashed cell phone and a pair of broken glasses. The blood was quickly matched and found to be IQ's. The broken glasses and cell phone were rushed to Maria's locked down house and confirmed by video to be IQ's.

Ely was in a pure panic mode when they left. "Mama, they hit IQ so hard! I'm so worried! He can't see very well without his glasses, and he was bleeding! Oh God, please help him!" Both Ely and Maria were sending up non-stop prayers.

Bill had been observing everything from up above and knew he had to give a little Level 2 assistance. He gave the 3 K-9s some extra superpowers and told Stumpy to give Sheba their location.

The "Team Badass" gang were now down to three people and one huge cat. They had been in contact with Harold at Microdots and found out about the failed drone search. They lied a little bit and told him they had been in contact with Chief Danny and would return home. They had a group meeting and figured that the kidnappers must have a base somewhere in the area, but out of The Villages. They had even seen the black FBI drones in the far distance searching back and forth. Suddenly, Sheba yowled loudly. She had heard from Stumpy.

"Vickie, it's me. Where are you? We need help. They hit IQ and me, and we were both knocked out. They have a revolver and a big club. We are in a green van, and they stopped after going down a bumpy road. It looks like we are under a dense stand of big trees. They have three really big drones that they are getting ready. There are also three huge suitcases."

"Damn them to Level 3, Jim. We will find them and take them out. It's going to get ugly! I will tear them to pieces for hurting you and IQ."

"Vickie, let's ask the K-9s for help. Maybe they can get away from their handlers."

"Good idea, Jim."

Saber, Lance and Chopper were resting at the police headquarters after a long day of searching, when suddenly, they all jumped up and headed for the door to the back fenced in area where they always did their business before heading out on patrol. The handlers thought it was a little odd, but they opened the door and left it ajar so the dogs could come in when they finished, just as they normally would. The officers were all talking about the kidnapping, and after about 10 minutes they realized that the dogs should have returned long ago. A check of the fenced in area showed no sign of them. They quickly checked the security cameras which also record any activity around the whole headquarters and saw an amazing sight. Saber and Lance had taken fast running starts and had run straight up the 15 foot high fence and over the top. They knew the Malinois were extremely athletic, but this looked otherworldly. Now in a panic, they looked for Chopper. Weighing over 100 pounds and being a little less athletic, they thought there was no way he could do that, but they were wrong. He had run up a side wall and landed on a covered dumpster. From there he leaped up, got a foothold on the fence and disappeared over the top of the fence. The officers were staring at the screen in disbelief, and another screen showed all three dogs running flat out and far faster than they believed possible, disappearing into the distance.

"Oh Shit, Chief Turner will have our asses for this! Get your gear on and let's find them quick! What the Hell is going on?"

By the time the officers got in the EV patrol vans, the dogs were over 2 miles away and running at a good 40 mph. Several walkers, bikers and golf cart drivers couldn't believe their eyes. People said it must have been the extra happy hour drinks they had, because nobody believed their stories.

The "Team Badass" gang were trying to decide which way to search. They knew the kidnappers were outside the main search area and under cover somewhere, so they were either in a probably abandoned building or in dense overgrowth where the van couldn't be seen. Suddenly Sheba went crazy, meowing and screeching with joy. Chopper, Lance and Saber came into view running flat out. They came to a sliding stop and weren't even panting. Sheba was greeting them all and rubbing all over them. The team greeted them all.

"Sheba, did you call them here somehow?"

Three nods of the head yes.

"Can you explain what happened to Stumpy and IQ, and tell them we need their help?"

Three more nods yes. In a little while all three dogs were growling and baring their teeth. Someone had hurt their friend Stumpy and his owner, IQ. They were out for blood.

Ben said, "Let's get off the main road and onto those side trails so we can search more territory on the outskirts of The Villages." They got the whole gang off the road before the patrol vans were even close.

Wallace and Cory launched their first drone with the ransom demand note on the outside of the huge suitcase. It asked for $5 million dollars in actual unmarked cash in 50 and 100 dollar bills with no tracking devices attached of any kind. If they found a tracking device or something or someone tracking the drone, they would kill the boy and the dog. The drone was flown under the trees and then under the power lines which interrupted any tracking signals. About two miles later, they saw a command center on their camera and flew in towards it to land. As luck would have it, Chief Danny Turner was there and read the note. He was absolutely livid, but he called Harold at Microdots and explained. Harold told him no problem, he would get the cash within the hour, as he knew lots of important people. The cash was rounded up and delivered to the command center in less than an hour. Danny had it packed into the suitcase and hit the return button. He wanted in the worst way to track the drone, as he thought the kidnappers may kill his boy anyway. Maybe this would buy them a little time at least, and they could visually observe which way the drone was headed. He notified the FBI drone, but they were miles away in a different search area. Danny was beside himself. He knew the whole family would be devastated if anything happened to IQ. He knew Ely and Maria would be trainwrecks if anything bad happened. He decided to contact Maria and update her.

She said, "Danny, you find them and you kill those bastards!" She told him that even his Dad, BD, was out searching in his golf cart and carrying a 12 gauge bullpup shotgun. Sunny had tried to stop him, but he dearly loved his genius grandson.

Danny thought, "My God, he is pushing 90 years of age, but I know better than to try to talk him out of searching."

Wallace and Cory were chuckling when they knew the drone was returning. This was the tricky part of the operation. They had it fly under the powerlines and then to the area under dense oak trees where the other two identical drones were waiting. They brought down the money drone and sent out the two identical drones with identical suitcases packed with newspapers. One was very slowly sent back to the original landing area at the command center, and one was programmed to slowly fly past that area and to a landing area a mile past there. They looked in the suitcase and all was well, there were only beautiful green 50 and 100 dollar bills. They couldn't detect any tracking devices with their handheld scanners, so they headed back to the hidden cabin where they had stashed IQ and Stumpy.

Stumpy had a very heavy rope attached to his collar and to an eyebolt fastened into the wall. IQ was tied down to a chair next to him. IQ told Stumpy to chew on the rope whenever the two bastards weren't watching. Stumpy made good progress when Wallace and Cory were out retrieving the ransom, and when he heard them returning he sat up to hide the progress.

"Team BadAss" and the three dogs were still searching along the outskirts, and it was nearing evening when they came upon a small house. Christy recognized it as the home of Albert Johnson, one of IQ's favorite employees. They spotted him bringing down a small drone as they pulled up. He was surprised when he saw the three kids, a massive cat and three dogs.

Albert recognized them and said, "Aren't you IQ's sister and two cousins? What are you doing all the way out here? There is dangerous stuff happening."

"We are searching for the kidnappers, Mr. Johnson. Have you seen anything suspicious out this way?"

Albert said, "Yes, on this last flight, I think I saw a van like they have been searching for pull into that old road near the dilapidated cabin by the big lake over an hour ago. Take a look here."

Ben, Lea and Christy looked at the video and knew he had found the hideout. "Mr. Johnson, you may have solved the kidnapping and saved IQ's life! We have to go right now! Please call Chief Turner and Harold at Microdots and tell them it's the cabin at the lake. Tell them to hurry."

"OK kids, please be careful!"

The kids hustled towards the cabin at top speed hoping they wouldn't be too late.

They discussed a plan to attack from three directions using Ben, Christy and the dogs. Sheba would be the back up, and Lea would patch up whoever needs it.

Wallace and Cory brought in the huge suitcase and opened it. They wanted to roll in all the money, it looked so good. They zipped it back closed and planned their next step.

IQ said, "I can get you 10 times that amount, if you just let us go. I won't tell anyone where you went. We are so far out, you can be many miles away before anyone shows up."

Wallace just laughed and said, "Sorry kid, you know too much."

This is when IQ knew he was going to die. All he could think about was Ely and how devastated she would be. He didn't pray for himself, he only prayed that God would give her a good life. She deserved it. Oh, how he loved her! He also prayed for his dad and mom, his sister, cousins, aunt and uncle and his Grandma and Grandpa Turner. They would all be heartbroken.

When the fake drones started to return to the command center, Danny didn't know what to make of it. One landed, and one flew past and was seen by other searchers about a mile from them. Danny rushed to the drone and opened the suitcase, only to find old newspapers. They got a call that searchers had found the other drone, and it too contained only old newspapers. Danny was so frustrated that he started screaming at his officers. "You backtrack and find them! Get moving, damn it! Search all night if you have to! They have to be within a two or three mile radius."

Suddenly, Danny's phone rang, and he saw it was from Albert Johnson. He remembered IQ telling him about giving Albert a job and what a nice person he was.

"Chief Turner, this is Albert Johnson. I work for your son, and his sister and two cousins were just here with three big dogs and a huge cat. They said to tell you to come to the cabin at the lake and to hurry."

"Thank you Albert, thank you."

The next call Albert made was to Harold at Microdots, and he relayed the same information. Within minutes, at least 100 drones were launched and headed toward the area of the cabin. Harold notified the FBI who immediately turned their manned drone in that direction, but they were still miles away.

Ben, Christy and Lea arrived at the cabin and approached the front. The dogs started to work their way around to the back through heavy underbrush. Christy couldn't get a good view through the small front window and started to work her way through the heavy growth to the side window. Ben quietly tried the front door, but it was locked. He put the new shock/bang stick on maximum.

He whispered to Sheba, "Jump on the window when I hit the front door knob."

Sheba made three head nods. Christy finally got around to the side window and saw IQ tied to the chair and Stumpy with a heavy rope on his collar. She quickly, but quietly, unzipped her shoulder bag.

Inside, Wallace told Cory to take care of their little problem child while he loaded the airboat with the cash. Then they had to leave the area as soon as possible. Stumpy was enraged and wanted to kill those bastards. Cory pulled out his .38 and said, "Sorry kid, but you heard the boss."

He pointed the .38 at IQ who had his eyes closed praying for Ely to not grieve too much and to have a good life. He had put her in his will, and she would be rich beyond her wildest imagination. She had no idea that he had included her in his will.

Ben said, "Now Sheba, hit the window!"

Sheba jumped as Ben pressed the bang stick against the doorknob and hit the button. The doorknob exploded inward and flew across the room as Sheba crashed against the window cracking the glass. The combined noises caused Cory to jerk the trigger and completely miss IQ by a couple of inches. Ben then crashed against the door at full speed with his shoulder, but the door was barred, and he injured his shoulder.

Cory thought, "Damn, the cops are here!"

He re-aimed the .38, but Stumpy saw his chance and lunged with all his weight and might, tearing the rope and heading for Cory with his huge mouth wide open and growling loudly. Cory took a snap shot and hit Stumpy in his artificial foot, causing him to howl in pain. Another shot hit Stumpy in the side, but the "Invisi-Shield" took the hit and spread it out around his body. Stumpy went down, but he was in pain and shock. Cory knew he had only two bullets left. Ben had recharged the bang stick and blew the hinges off the front door. He would get in one way or another. Sheba hit the window again, this time fully breaking the glass and cutting herself.

Cory took aim again, but just fractions of a second before he pulled the trigger, there was a loud booming sound outside the side window, and his shoulder was hit with a .45 caliber bullet, knocking his aim off. The .38 went flying out of his hand and slid across the floor towards the rear exit. Christy was standing outside the window with grandpa's old Colt .45 from the Korean war that he had inherited from old PopPop. She was using a two handed grip in a perfect Weaver stance taught to her by her father and grandpa. The .38 bullet had hit IQ in the side, breaking a rib and going clean through his side, luckily missing any vital organs. There was a lot of blood loss though, and Christy was enraged when she saw it. She shot again and hit Cory in the leg, each shot being punctuated with a vile curse.

Wallace had hurried back from loading the airboat after hearing more than one shot and the bang stick going off. He wondered what the Hell was going on. When he ducked down to come in the low back door, he saw Cory get spun around and saw the .38 fly across the floor. Wallace grabbed the .38, but realized there was only one shot left. He backed out of the room, and he was tempted to take a shot at the figure outside the window. Christy saw him and took a shot at him, just barely missing him and taking a chunk of wood out of the doorframe. Another very close shot scared him out of the room for good. He decided to leave Cory and have the loot all for himself.

Ben had finally kicked the door in and saw Cory leaning up against the wall bleeding like a stuck pig. He jabbed him with the 3 foot long bang stick, but he forgot to put it on shock mode. It blew a hole clean through Cory's side, about an inch in diameter, just as another round from the .45 hit him in the chest. As he was going down, he got hit with another round in the abdomen. Christy climbed through the broken window, getting cut up on the broken glass. Another vile curse came from Christy as she stood over Cory and put one into his forehead, spattering his brains out the back all over the floor. That was round number 7, so she dropped the empty magazine out and rammed another one in, slamming the slide forward to put another round in the chamber.

Christy paused just a second to spit on Cory, "That's for trying to kill my brother! Ben, let's get that other Son of a Bitch." She pulled out the switchblade and slid it across the floor toward IQ in the chair.

Ben hollered, "Lea, come in the front door, cut IQ loose and fix him up. Hurry, Hurry!" He also paused for just a second to deposit some spit on Cory. He said, "Rot in Hell, shithead!"

Lea hustled into the cabin from behind a tree where Ben had ordered her to stay until they cleared the room. She was shocked by the carnage in the room, but hurried over to IQ, who seemed to be in a lot of pain. She quickly opened her trauma kit and got out the newest "Quick Clot" product. It was made of the latest type of hemostatic gel, which worked in mere seconds. She applied antiseptic and the "Quick Clot." IQ was in a lot of pain, but recognized Lea.

"I knew the team would come," he whispered.

She quickly cut him loose with the switchblade, but told him not to move around, as she suspected he had a broken rib or internal damage.

Wallace had quickly headed down the trail towards the dock, but he stopped short when he heard loud growling sounds. He looked around to see Chopper blocking the path to the dock, with Saber on one side and with Lance on the other. He only had one shot left in the 38, but maybe he could use it on the biggest dog and threaten the others with the empty gun. All of a sudden, he heard a terrible, loud, high pitched screeching sound above him and made the mistake of looking up. Out of the dark shadows of the oak tree sprang 45 pounds of enraged Sheba, all 18 razor sharp claws and a mouthful of teeth. She landed on his head and chest with her fangs embedded in his scalp and her claws tearing at his face and chest.

"You shot my friends, you bastard! I'll make hamburger meat out of you!"

Her claws were ripping at Wallace and tore into his left eyelid, cheek and chest.

The attack was so fast and vicious, that he barely had time to raise his arms. His only thought was to shoot the huge massive cat off of him. It was only seconds until she would take an eye out. When he started to raise the gun, Saber saw his chance and leaped for his arm, grabbing his forearm and causing a wild shot which ripped through Sheba's fur on her back. This caused her to release her grip and retreat back up the oak tree. Now Lance attacked and grabbed his ankle with Chopper following suit on the other ankle. Bleeding profusely from the head and face, Wallace knew he was in serious trouble. He tried to switch the gun to his free hand so he could beat on the attacking dogs, but he dropped it on the ground. Ben and Christy appeared from the back of the cabin and just watched as the dogs used Wallace as a chew toy.

Ben said, "Should we call them off?"

Christy laughed and said, "Let them have a little fun, after all, they ran all this way."

The dogs finally dragged big Wallace to the ground, and he begged the two kids for help.

Christy walked over, smiled, and said, "I'll give you help, the way you tried to give my brother help." She raised the .45 and put a shot into his forehead. They let the dogs continue their attack.

Finally, Stumpy came to and heard from Bill up in Level 2.

"Come on big guy, have a little fun. I'm going to give you a considerable amount of extra biting power. Go hop over and get some revenge. Don't worry, IQ will fix that foot up again."

Stumpy got to his 3 good feet, hopped over to Cory and snapped his lower leg in half like a twig. Then he hopped outside and did the same thing to Wallace's legs, impressing even the K-9s. Christy and Ben called the K-9s off and asked them to sit and wait. All this action took only minutes, and they could hear all kinds of drones and EVs coming from every direction. They ran back into the cabin to check on IQ and found Lea applying a type of moldable cast which would keep his ribs from moving around and causing possible internal damage. All three of them and all 4 dogs were covered in blood. Ben's shoulder had been dislocated and hung at an odd angle. Christy was all cut up from the glass and bleeding. Lea quickly put a sling on Ben's arm.

Christy said, "Stumpy, please contact Sheba, I think she's hurt."

Stumpy mentally called out, "Sheba, Vickie, I'm OK, Come into the cabin."

It took a couple of minutes, but Sheba walked in covered in blood and also bleeding from her back. She was not a happy cat until she found out everyone was going to be OK. Lea patched her up with some "Quick Clot" until a Vet could look her over. Stumpy and Sheba had a happy reunion, but they looked each other over.

"Damn, Stumpy, your fake paw is hanging loose, your head has a big lump and you're covered in blood."

"You don't look so good yourself, Miss Dracula. You're covered in blood also, and I'm really hungry."

"When aren't you, big guy? I'm so glad to see you."

Suddenly the cabin and the whole area around it for a hundred yards lit up like it was 12 noon. Swat teams, FBI teams and about 50 policemen from Chief Turner's command had surrounded the cabin in seconds. Danny came charging into the cabin with 5 of his men with guns drawn. He couldn't believe his eyes as he looked around the small room. It looked like a war zone. He first looked for IQ, and Lea told him that IQ needed an immediate air ambulance to the nearest hospital. He almost broke down when he saw that IQ was alive and weakly called out, "Daddy, the team saved me."

He had previously arranged for air transport, and IQ was on his way quickly with his Dad telling him he would be at the hospital to see him very soon. Then he checked out the other three kids, Stumpy and Sheba, and ordered them to go on a second large transport to the hospital and drop the pets off at the Vet. Lea wasn't injured, but she sure wasn't going to argue with Uncle Danny in his state of mind.

He said, "I'll talk to you kids later." He looked relieved, but didn't look very happy with them.

"Oh, Shit, I forgot to call Maria and Ashley!"

Maria and Ely were still sending up constant prayers when the phone rang. Maria answered quickly and had the phone on speaker when Danny said that IQ had been shot, but would be OK and was on the way to the hospital. All Ely heard was the word shot, and she turned white and collapsed against the couch. Danny said that Stumpy was also shot, but he was hit in the vest and had his paw damaged, but would be OK. He told Maria to go off lockdown and meet him at the hospital later. He said the other kids were slightly injured, but would be fine. He told her that Sheba needed to go to the Vet also. He told Maria to call Ashley and that he had tons of work to do at the crime scene and would meet them at the hospital.

Ely came to with Maria holding her. She whispered, "My IQ, not my IQ, please God!"

"Ely, he will be OK and is at the hospital. Stumpy and Sheba were also injured and are at the Vet. We'll go see IQ first, as soon as we call Ashley. We better call Grandpa, and Grandma too."

Chapter 16
The Aftermath

Andy arrived at the cabin and got a quick briefing from Danny. He asked Danny a couple of times, "Captain, are you absolutely sure all the kids are OK? It really does look like a war zone here."

"Yes Lieutenant, they were a little beat up and covered with blood, but should be fine. IQ took the worst of it, but Lea patched him up, and they all should be arriving within minutes to the closest hospital. I don't mind saying that I was terrified all day."

"Me too, I was getting calls from Ashley every 5 minutes when she saw Ben and Lea were missing."

"Andy, have the CSI guys take pictures from all angles, inside and outside, and instruct all the officers and FBI to not touch anything. This is going to be major news for weeks. There are some very odd wounds, and we have to debrief those kids as soon as we can. Call me Danny tonight, this is our family we are dealing with. This is going to be crazy to figure out what happened. This clown on the floor certainly messed with the wrong family."

Danny and the CSI gang found 6 shell casings in the underbrush and one on the cabin floor. Christy must have shot through the window 6 times and put the 7th shot into the guy on the floor after climbing through the window. She must have gotten all cut up on the glass shards left in the window frame, as they found some blood on the window frame and the glass shards. Andy came in and told Danny that they found one shell casing outside near the body of the big guy. He was shot through the forehead, and that was probably the kill shot. The rest of the body was all badly torn up on the face, chest and scalp, and he was guessing it was Sheba that did that damage. The lower legs and right arm were all chewed up, and both lower legs were snapped almost in two. He had never seen anything like it. It was almost certainly the three K-9s that chewed him up, but there is no way they could crush bones like that.

They looked at each and said almost in unison, "Stumpy! It had to be Stumpy!"

"Andy, look at this guy on the floor here. His one leg looks the same as the guy outside. Check out that hole through his side. It's about an inch in diameter. I'm thinking that Ben used the combo bang/shock stick. It looks like he blew the doorknob in and tried to knock the door in with his body. He had an injured shoulder. When he found the door was barred, he blew the two hinges off, and the door just rotated around that crossbar after that. We found where two bullets hit the floor, possibly after striking Stumpy. There were two more, one missed IQ to the left of the chair and one hit him in the side." Danny's voice suddenly got all emotional as he thought how close they had come to losing IQ.

"Danny, they were using an old .38 revolver with only a 5 round capacity. It was found near the body outside. One bullet we may never locate, and all five shell casings are in the gun. I think Sheba and Stumpy got really pissed off to inflict wounds like we found. The coroner is going to have a real job working with these two bodies."

One of Danny's top SWAT officers came in and reported finding the ransom money in an EV airboat at the dock. He said he could handle the rest of the work and they should hurry to the hospital to check on the kids. The K-9 officers had shown up for their dogs, and the coroner's office was on the way for the bodies. He would make sure enough pictures were taken, all evidence was collected and the crime scene secured all night. They would make sure none of the press got close and would make sure no info was given out until tomorrow. He told Danny and Andy that he had assigned two men on guard duty at the hospital for IQ's room.

Andy and Danny used one of the high speed police pursuit drones and raced to the hospital at top speed. Ashley, Maria and Ely had arrived previously, but IQ had been taken into surgery before they were able to see him. X-Rays were taken and showed just how close the bullet came to major organ damage. Lea's quick work on stopping the blood flow, the use of a compression bandage and the moldable cast may have saved his life. The doctors and nurses all praised her quick action and skill, but she just wanted to see IQ for herself. They were fixing his broken rib, giving him a transfusion and repairing the internal damage. He would be out of surgery in a short time. Modern medical techniques were amazing in the 2080's, and if you could get to a hospital in time, you would have an excellent chance of survival.

Danny and Andy came running in and asked about IQ. The nurses said he would be out of surgery shortly and that the rest of the family were in the small chapel. She said they would be notified as soon as he could be seen. Danny and Andy found everyone in the chapel talking quietly, except Ely, who was kneeling at the front praying non-stop. Ashley grabbed Andy in a tight hug and wouldn't let go. Ben and Lea joined in. Ben had his arm in a sling, and Lea was still in her bloody clothes. Andy looked them over, and Ben said they popped his dislocated shoulder back in and he would be fine in a few days. Lea said she wasn't hurt at all, it was all IQ, Christy and Shebas' blood.

"You kids scared the hell out of us. Were you trying to make our hair turn white?"

"Daddy, we're sorry, but we had to find IQ. We all made a pact for 'Team Badass' to protect each other," said Lea.

Danny said, "Christy honey, are you alright?"

Her clothes were covered in blood, and she had about a dozen bandages on her arms and legs. She said, "Daddy, they came so close to killing our IQ. It would have been another half second if I hadn't taken that first shot."

She started to shake like a leaf, and Danny sat down, pulled her close and held her tight. She was tough as nails and never cried since she was a little girl, but she was really shaken up this time. He rocked her back and forth slowly, just a little and told her how very proud he was of her. She rested there with her head on his chest for quite a while. Maria, who had been holding Ely's hand, came over to hug Danny and Christy. She gave Danny the "go easy on her" look, with a head tilt and a raised index finger.

Ely got up and came over to Danny and said, "Papa, they saved my IQ. I wish I could have helped them. I knew God would save the angel he sent me, I just knew it!"

Danny said, "I know you would have helped, but I'm glad you stayed safe with Mama T. You and IQ were the only ones who knew what the kidnappers looked like." He decided to ask Maria about the angel remark when he got a chance.

The nurse came in and told them that all went very well, and they were bringing IQ back to a private room. She didn't want more than two people at a time to visit and only for five minutes each until tomorrow. They all looked at each other and picked Danny and Maria to go in first. IQ looked very small and very pale in that hospital bed. He was hooked up to oxygen, a fluid drip line and several other gadgets for pulse and BP. He was awake and recognized his parents. He had a concussion and bandaged temple as well as the bandaged left side. The nurse had warned everybody to not hug him or upset him.

He softly said, "Mom and Dad!"

They both gave him a kiss on the cheek. He was surprised, because his Dad never did that. His Mom was teary eyed. They must have been very worried. He asked about the other kids and then about Stumpy and Sheba. After hearing that everyone would be OK, he asked his Dad to come closer.

IQ grabbed his hand and softly said, "Daddy, please promise me not to holler at the gang. They really did save my life. Promise me you won't holler or stay mad at them."

Danny's expression softened and he said, "I promise! I love you Son."

"I love you and you too, Mom. Can I see Ely? She must have been so worried."

"Sure Son, we'll send her in next, and yes, she was praying non-stop for you all day. You rest well tonight. I will have two armed guards outside at all times." When they left the room, Maria started bawling and was hugging Danny. She made sure to wipe her eyes and smile before they turned the corner into the chapel.

Ely asked Christy to come in with her, so it wouldn't take as long for everyone to see IQ and possibly tire him out too much. Christy hung back a little when Ely went in. She knew how close those two were. Ely's eyes were flowing with tears as she ran to the bed. "IQ, IQ!" That was all she could get out as she kissed him and held his hand. She sat on the chair next to the bed, laid her head next to his and whispered how much she loved him over and over. Christy smiled from across the room and finally walked over catching IQ's eye.

"Christy, You look like someone dragged you through a briar patch. Come here and give me a sister smooch." She gave him a kiss on the cheek as Ely tried to dry her eyes.

"Your blood pressure and pulse went way up when Ely arrived," she teased.

"It always does. Seriously though, you and the rest of the gang saved my life. You've always looked out for me. I love you Sis."

"I love you too Bro. Our five minutes are up Ely. Give that guy one last kiss until morning." She did just that, but it took quite a while.

Ashley and Lea went in next. IQ told Aunt Ashley the same thing about the gang saving his life. "Lea, the nurses told me if it wasn't for you, I might not have made it. I love you cousin Lea. You will make a top notch nurse, doctor or whatever you want to be someday."

A little embarrassed by the praise, Lea said, "It took the whole gang IQ."

"Aunt Ashley, come here, I want to ask you something." He took her hand and asked her to promise not to holler or get mad at the gang, as he wouldn't have been here without them. She promised and gave him a kiss on the cheek. She hugged Lea on the way out and told her how very proud she was of her.

The head nurse asked the last two to shorten their visit, as IQ looked very tired. So Ben and Uncle Andy went in for just a short look.

IQ looked at Ben and asked if he got hit with the same drone that ran over him.

"Oh boy, he's still got a sense of humor," Ben said with a grin. "Listen IQ, I called the Vet and those two monster pets are going to be fine, but Stumpy will need a new paw."

"Great, thanks Ben." IQ made Uncle Andy promise to not holler at the gang and he agreed.

IQ fell asleep as soon as they headed for the door and was out all night. On the way back to the waiting room, Andy hugged Ben and told him he was very proud of him and the gang. Andy and Danny got together and started having a discussion about debriefing the kids, but they decided to wait until IQ could participate. They would wait until morning. They saw Lea, Ben and Christy whispering to each other over in a corner and glancing their way. They thought maybe the kids were worried about getting screamed at for going out on their own, but they had made a promise to IQ and would go very easy on them. Actually the kids were getting their story straight about what happened since there were some brutal wounds on the two dead kidnappers. They were a little worried about the two headshots Christy made, but the kidnappers well deserved them.

Two armed SWAT guards were positioned outside the door making sure nobody entered except family or hospital staff. Andy gave orders to particularly keep the news media away. They would have a field day with this story anyway.

Chapter 17
The News Media

Harold at Microdots was notified by Chief Danny from the hospital that IQ had been rescued. He told him that IQ had been injured, but would recover and that he would supply the details in the morning. He told Harold that they could go off of the Priority 3 Lockdown but to give the press no information. Harold hit the all clear code which shut off the Priority 3 red flashing lights switching them all to steady green. He made a short announcement about IQ, and loud cheering erupted throughout the entire facility. There were high fives and hugs all over the place. Olive was so relieved that she grabbed Harold and kissed him right on the lips. They danced around like a couple of kids. Harold was thinking about how great that kiss felt and hoped for more in the future. If only he had the guts to ask her out. But what if she turned him down? He would feel like a fool.

Eva had spent hours fending off the more and more insistent questions from the press. At least the Priority 3 Level had helped. Now it was lifted, but armed guards were still stationed outside and letting nobody in. She called Ely and told her that she loved her and how relieved she was that IQ was going to be alright.

Someone had captured the whole kidnapping on a door cam video and leaked it to the press even before the police found out about it. The nightly news replayed it over and over. The lead in to the news said, "Boy genius, Dean Benjamin Turner, Owner of Microdots Company, brutally assaulted and kidnapped in broad daylight by three armed men. His girlfriend, Miss Elyssia Simmons, narrowly escaped the kidnapping by sprinting down the sidewalk while sounding some type of unusual alarm. Turner's pet dog was also viciously assaulted and taken. Huge searches initiated by hundreds of company drones were to no avail. Reports are coming in of a huge police and FBI presence near Lake Agarro. Stay tuned."

They found a short video of grandpa and played it, saying, "Retired, highly decorated Police Chief, BD Turner, age 89, searches for his beloved grandson via golf cart, armed with a 12 gauge shotgun. Woe be to the kidnappers if he locates them."

Another clip showed the entire school football team wearing their jersey tops, searching in pairs and armed with baseball bats, pipes and clubs. They had been organized by star player, big Joe Hill, who told the press that IQ was one of them, and they would search all night if necessary. Someone had captured a video clip of the 3 K-9's running at an impossible speed toward the lake area. "K-9's seen racing towards the general area of the lake at top speed. Did they help with the rescue, and if so, where are their handlers?"

Ely could only watch the kidnapping video once before breaking into tears when she saw how hard Cory hit IQ and how very close Wallace had come to grabbing her. Danny and Andy wanted to know who leaked the video to the press, but they couldn't get any quick answers. The rest of the family were appalled watching the video. Christy, Ben and Lea were really pissed off and were glad they had snuck out. They were discussing the rescue when suddenly, Christy started shaking again and went to her Mom asking to be held.

Maria held her close on a recliner saying, "It will be alright sweetheart. You saved your brother, and we are all so very proud of you."

Maria thought she might have PTSD, very common among police officers after traumatic events. She would ask Danny about it as soon as she saw him. They had people who were very good at dealing with that. She held Christy for a long time, stroking her hair and kissing her forehead just like when she was a little girl.

Danny and Andy held a very brief press conference saying that IQ had been rescued, but he was in the hospital after being wounded by the kidnappers. He will be OK after the very quick treatment by his rescuers and the hospital. Two of the kidnappers had been killed during the rescue and the driver of the white van arrested. Because of the very complex operation required and the very unusual rescue, it would take them until late morning to give a more detailed report. They were asked to please respect the privacy of the family. They would take no questions until the late morning press conference. Somehow, a picture of the three kids was taken in the hospital and leaked to the press. This too made the late night news.

The headlines read, "Turner boy rescued, but seriously injured! His twin sister Christy and twin cousins Ben and Lea were seen at the hospital covered in blood and gore and appear to be somehow involved. Possible injuries to Ben and Christy. Where is Turner's pet dog that was cruelly attacked? Don't miss the press conference tomorrow!"

Danny and Andy spent hours back at the cabin going over the evidence again. They were pretty certain that the whole event played out like they first thought. The only thing that worried them were the two shots to the heads of the kidnappers. It almost looked unnecessary, but they would debrief the kids in the early morning at the hospital if IQ was feeling up to it. His input would be invaluable. They talked about how to handle the press conference and decided not to take any bullshit questions, those usually coming from a certain 2 leftwing bleeding heart liberals. These were the ones who always asked about excessive use of force and police brutality. They had to explain the event exactly how it unfolded. Danny called the whole gang and told them to be at the hospital at exactly 8 AM, Maria, Ashley and Ely included.

"Andy, darn it, we promised IQ not to holler at the kids, but I have to say something. They took off without saying anything, took weapons out of our houses and didn't tell us where they were all day. They almost got themselves and their two pets killed. Good grief!"

"Danny, we have to go easy on them. Maria said she thinks Christy may have PTSD, and the other kids look a little shell shocked also. Ashley told me that poor Ely has been crying on and off for hours."

At 7:30 AM, the whole family arrived at the hospital and were amazed to see IQ sitting up in a chair and using a borrowed cellphone. He said, "Harold, gotta go, the whole family is here."

Ely ran over to him, knelt on the floor and kissed him, saying, "Oh IQ, my IQ!"

He told her she was better for him than any medicine in the hospital. She smoothed his hair out and softly touched his injured temple with tears in her eyes.

"I brought you your spare pair of glasses, if it doesn't hurt to wear them," she said.

He replied, "Miss Ely, I love you more than you can ever imagine! That was so very thoughtful."

After the rest of the family greeted him, Danny had them all go into a meeting room and sat the kids in a row with Ashley, Maria and Andy standing on one side. Andy was rubbing his face and brow and frowning. Danny started to pace back and forth. He was rubbing his brow, waving his arms around, occasionally pointing at the kids with both hands and mumbling to himself. The kids' heads and eyes were going back and forth like they were watching a slow motion pickleball game. They were all thinking that they would be grounded for life.

Suddenly a voice softly said, "Papa!"

Danny stopped and turned and said, "Yes Ely?"

"Papa, please don't holler at them, they saved my angel!"

Suddenly, all Danny's anger disappeared, and he gestured at all four kids to come get a hug. "Ely's right, how could I stay mad at anybody who saved our IQ. But Andy and I need to know exactly what happened yesterday. We need to get IQ in here if it's ok with the nurses."

The nurses told them that IQ was making an amazing recovery, but they should wheel him in and keep him no longer than a half hour. Ely literally sprinted down the hallway, helped IQ into a wheelchair and pushed him back to the room.

IQ found out that it was Albert who found the kidnappers' van by using the small drone that he had gifted to him, and he just smiled and shook his head. After finding out Microdots sent up a hundred drones in a search pattern and did a successful Priority 3 lockdown, he was very pleased. He smiled about Albert and the "Badass Gang" coming to the rescue when hundreds of policemen, the FBI, all kinds of drones and searchers on the ground couldn't find him. Danny asked about the exact way the rescue went down. They told him about the front door assault by Ben and window assault by Sheba. They went over how they heard Wallace tell Cory to kill IQ and head to the airboat where he would stash the ransom. What pissed them off was the fact that they laughed about it, not even caring if they took a life. They told about Stumpy getting shot twice as he lunged at Cory. Christy told them about shooting through the window just a fraction of a second before Cory pulled the trigger, then hitting him again in the leg. Then she saw Wallace pick up the gun and she fired two shots at him. Ben got through the front door after she hit Cory again twice. They both said he was tough and wouldn't go down, so Ben jabbed him with the shock/bang stick, but forgot to set it on shock and blew a hole in his side. Christy said she climbed through the window and Cory was still trying to get up. He made a grab for Ben's bangstick, so Christy used her last round to finish him off. IQ was listening with great interest and knew they had changed the story a little bit.

When Danny asked him if he remembered it going down that way, he said, "Yes Daddy, that Cory was a mean, tough SOB and tried to grab Ben's bangstick even as he was lying on the floor on his back. Christy had to stop the threat and she did. I was in a lot of pain, but I saw the whole thing. They saved my life and then Lea was called in from outside to patch me up and did an awesome job. I don't know what happened outside."

Danny and Andy exchanged glances and both shrugged. They knew IQ never lied about anything in his life. It must have gone down just like they claimed.

Danny asked about the K-9s and how they found the gang so fast. Ben thought that possibly Sheba was able to contact them somehow. They just showed up running at top speed. Danny was wondering how they got away from their handlers miles away and got to them so bloody fast. He would look into that.

Ben and Christy told Danny about going outside and finding Wallace all torn up on his head, face and chest. They had heard a shot fired and found out later that he shot Sheba. The three dogs were using Wallace as a chew toy, with one dog on his shooting arm and one on each leg. They said the dogs pulled him to the ground, and he tried to point the gun at Chopper. That's when Christy shot him. They told him of Stumpy limping outside and snapping Wallace's lower legs. Going back inside to see if Lea needed any help, they noticed Cory's one leg was broken and assumed Stumpy did that also. Then the cabin lit up all around and you came charging in. They only told two little white lies about the headshots, and with IQ backing them up, no one would ever be able to say different.

Andy and Danny had a discussion and everything agreed with their findings. Now they needed to have a very long press conference.

Suddenly Christy said, "Daddy, I don't feel well." She had started shaking like a leaf again, and Danny knew she was reliving the shooting.

He and Maria rushed over to hold her and tell her everything was going to be alright. Lea went out and asked the nurses if they had anything to help, and they gave her some meds to help Christy relax and calm down. IQ had to get some rest and was wheeled back with Ely sticking to him like glue. She asked the nurses if she could please stay in the room while IQ rested. She sat by the bed for hours while IQ napped, holding and occasionally kissing his hand the whole time. The nurses all smiled to each other, knowing quite a bit about young love.

Danny and Andy were right about the press having a field day. They told the huge crowd of reporters to not shout out questions until they finished talking. They told the long story from the beginning of the kidnapping until it's ending with the rush of IQ to the hospital. Reporters were furiously recording and writing questions down that they wanted answers about. Many of the questions were about how three young teenagers were able to find the kidnappers location when hundreds of well trained police, FBI and massive flights of drones couldn't. Danny explained again about having to cover such a massive area and about the kidnappers' well executed plan. Danny praised Albert Johnson, a Microdots employee, who lived outside of The Villages and used his own personal drone to finally spot the switched out van heading to the lake. He told them that the three kids had successfully reasoned that the kidnappers' location must be on the outskirts somewhere, and they came upon Albert's location by sheer luck.

There were many questions about how three kids, three K-9s and a huge cat could take down two grown men with a gun. Danny and Andy explained that Andy's son, Ben, was an intern with the police department and well versed in tactics and use of a shock/bangstick. They told of Andy's daughter, Lea, being a nursing intern with excellent skills and probably kept IQ from bleeding to death. Danny told about his daughter, Christy, also being an intern at the police department and of her extensive training with firearms, particularly the Colt .45 used that day. He explained a little of the history of the gun and how it was used to save his mother Sunny Turner's life way back in 2023.

The press wondered how the kids could sneak away to attempt a rescue, and Danny said they had gotten a good talking to about that. He had to explain again about the three K-9 dogs and the huge cat attacking Wallace, with him wounding Sheba and attempting to shoot Chopper, the German Shepherd, right before being shot by Christy. He said they were still investigating how the K-9's got out and found their way to the lake. It was a mystery at the moment. There were questions about Ely and the alarms that went off all over the city.

Danny explained that Ely was given a special locket from IQ two years ago and everything was programmed into it. This was its first use and hopefully its last. She activated it while running back to his house. They explained that both of the pets had been shot by the kidnappers, but they were being treated by a Vet and were expected to be OK.

Finally, the press was running out of questions and the session was breaking up, but a couple of them persisted about the shooting and whether it was necessary to kill the two kidnappers. Andy saw that Danny was getting ready to explode on them and interceded. He asked if they had children and pets. They both did. He asked how they would like it if one of their kids, while out innocently walking with their pet, got slammed across the side of their head with a gun, hard enough to cause a concussion, break glasses and put a gash deep enough for 6 stitches. Then their docile rescue pet would get clubbed hard enough to knock it senseless and be thrown into a van along with their tied up kid. Then have your kid get told later that he was going to die because he knew too much. Then have them laugh about it and shoot your beloved pet twice and your kid once, he or she only living because your kid's sister or brother was quick enough to shoot first and knock his aim off. Would you still let him shoot at your kid again or stop the threat? Would you like your other rescue pet shot in the back and the guy then try to shoot a police dog? Would you shoot him then to stop the threat after he attempts to point the gun at you?

He told them, "You candy asses get out of my sight."

Andy was slowly walking towards the reporters, and they left the area. Danny had never seen Andy explode like that, and he was sure something would be said in the newspaper or on the TV news.

Luckily, Danny was in charge, and he put his arm around Andy and said, "Easy big guy, let's go do some of our huge amount of paperwork. We also have to find out how those K-9s got loose. We also have to have a word with the protection detail that was supposed to watch IQ and Ely in the first place."

Danny was right, this story was huge and played constantly on TV with updates as the press uncovered more facts. They showed everything from the kidnapping until the leaked picture of the kids in the hospital covered in blood and gore. They found out which Vet treated Stumpy and Sheba and took multiple videos and pictures upon their release. The PETA people all over the country were particularly incensed when they saw Stumpy limping out with his bad leg missing its paw. The head Veterinarian came out and talked to the reporters, telling them that IQ, Ely and the other three kids were the same wonderful kids who had rescued the pets from the dogfighting ring quite a few months earlier in a very daring rescue. He slipped up and said they called themselves "Team Badass." He praised IQ for his efforts and contributions all over the state trying to make every shelter into a "No Kill" shelter. He told them Stumpy would be fitted with a new paw very soon. The Cat Ladies Society went crazy when they found out Sheba had been injured by the kidnappers.

When she slinked out next to Stumpy, he said, "Vickie, look at this, we're celebrities. I wonder if we are going to get special treats at home? I'm getting really hungry."

Vickie was laughing and said, "My God, you got hit over the head, shot twice and lost your paw, but you are still thinking about food. But actually, now that you mention it, maybe Christy has cooked up some of that delicious chicken she makes for me. Let's get on that special drone. Wow, we even have a police escort!"

As it turned out, there was not as much blowback about the kidnappers not surviving as Danny and Andy thought there would be. Only one reporter thought it was overkill, but the second one had actually done more research and refuted everything about the story. He reported that the kidnappers had been released after serving only half of their sentence and never should have been out of prison to cause more mayhem. He went over their previous records and found lengthy rap sheets on both of them. He discussed in length how the teenagers were the top 5 students in the class of 155 and about the many philanthropy projects IQ had undertaken even at this young age. He praised their amazing decisions and bravery under fire that even matched what fully trained police officers might do. He told the first reporter that "talk's cheap" when you aren't under fire. He finished off a rather lengthy column by saying that the world is better off with their demise.

At school, the kidnapping was discussed over and over. Phone texts, messages and calls were rampant. The school principal came into the classrooms to go over in detail what happened. To say the class was in awe of "Team Badass" would be an understatement. It was three days until Ely, Christy, Ben and Lea returned to class. Suddenly, they were the most popular kids in school. Christy thought that she would never get a date after they found out about her involvement, but she was wrong. Big Joe, the top athlete in the school, had always been interested in her and thought she was beautiful, but he was a little scared to ask her out. She went over to him and thanked him for organizing the search party composed of the football players that she had heard about. He told her that IQ was a good friend and that they wish they could have been at the cabin to help. He decided to tell her that he always wanted to ask her out and wondered if she would go with him for pizza some Friday night.

She looked up at him, hesitated for a second and surprised him by saying, "Sure, how about this Friday?" She even gave him one of her rare smiles and a wink. Joe was daydreaming the whole day after that.

Ely was surrounded by a bunch of girls who asked about IQ and about her close escape. They asked if they could see the locket that gave the alarm. Some were impressed with her speed while running away from the kidnappers. Ely was not used to being the center of attention, but it felt kind of good.

Ben got plenty of attention from the girls who asked how his shoulder was doing. His arm would still be in a sling for a couple more days. He was asked if he really did knock down and blast open a door to get into the cabin. He got a lot of attention from a pretty brunette who had caught his eye. He decided to ask her out when they were alone.

Lea, always very popular, had a lot of girls asking about her internship and how they could get into the nursing program. They asked her if she had been scared at the cabin, but she said her only thoughts were of getting to her cousin and fixing him up as soon as possible.

IQ was getting released from the hospital Saturday and had his personal ultra plush drone sent over. He had been busy making calls and setting up a couple of special appointments that he didn't want anyone to know about. He asked Harold and Olive to come in for a couple of hours in the afternoon to get him up to speed. He said he would enter from the roof as there were scads of people from the press still hanging around outside the complex who wanted to interview him. This way he could avoid most of them. He called two reporters with whom he had granted interviews in the past about his company. He said he would give them an exclusive one hour interview, as he knew them to be fair and not sensationalists. He told his mom and dad that he didn't need any help, but loved them so much for being so helpful to Ely, himself and the gang. When the drone landed on the roof of the hospital to pick him up, he got quite the surprise. Ely was waiting in the drone for him with open arms. The ride to Microdots was not too long, but the kisses were so good.

He said, "Ely, you're all I thought about the whole time during that ordeal. I love you so much."

She said to him, "I prayed for you so much! God granted me my angel back."

He thought it was an unusual comment, but he couldn't ask what she meant, because she was kissing him again and again. IQ told Ely that he had an appointment at the optometrist and a surprise appointment that he would tell her about later. He told her to meet him at his house later in the afternoon and mentioned about the reporter's interview and the meeting with Harold and Olive. It was going to be an action packed Saturday.

It would take weeks for the commotion to die down and until something else caught the presses' attention as usual.

Chapter 18
Life goes on, Mostly Good Years

IQ's first appointment was at the optometrist where he was fitted with the latest type of ultrathin contact lenses. He hated anyone even putting drops in his eyes, let alone inserting contacts, but he wanted to get away from wearing glasses once and for all. These were one month contacts, and the inserting turned out to be easier than he thought. He was amazed at his perfect 20-20 vision. His next appointment was at a regular beauty shop where he had his unruly red hair dyed to a reddish brown and tamed. He looked in the mirror and couldn't believe that he was actually looking at a reflection. He wondered what the team would say.

He quickly returned to Microdots and found that the two reporters had just arrived.

Eva did a double take, told him he looked great and that she was so happy he was OK.

IQ thanked her and took the two reporters on a quick tour of everything but the Class 3 section. He explained that very sensitive, top secret work was going on in that section for the government, and no one was allowed in except himself and his top two people. He sat down for a good interview and explained that he came very close to dying. An inch more would likely have hit vital organs. He explained again how amazing the rescue by 3 of the "Team Badass" gang and the 5 animals was. The interview went very well, and the writeups were very favorable. Harold and Olive were amazed at his new appearance and were thrilled with his quick recovery. He praised them for their Priority 3 lockdown and search efforts. He told them to have Albert Johnson report to his office first thing Monday afternoon when he arrived after school, as he had a nice surprise waiting for him. But he told them not to say why he wanted Albert in his office. His side was hurting a little bit, so he sat in his office and said a little prayer thanking God for saving him, Ely and the other three from more serious harm. He didn't know if the "Big Guy," as he called him, worried too much about animals, but he said a little prayer for all 5 animals involved anyway.

Bill was listening in Level 2 and highly approved. He would make sure this whole group had good luck on his watch from now on.

IQ called Ely and said he was on the way in his drone. He asked if everyone would be able to come and have a big feast. It would be his treat. He told her to tell his mom not to make anything and asked if they would invite Grandma Sunny and Grandpa BD to come if they felt up to it.

When IQ walked in everyone just stared at his new appearance. Ely spun him around to look at all sides and told him he looked amazing. She told him that she didn't know his eyes were so blue. She gave him one of her famous kisses. The rest of the family thought he looked two years older and heartily approved of the changes. Ely couldn't keep from looking at him and stayed close by him, gingerly hugging him and holding his hand.

Danny and Maria were thrilled, and Danny whispered, "Ely is all over him like a 'hobo on a ham sandwich.'"

Maria elbowed him and said, "Remember, it wasn't too, too long ago we were like that. I'll see you later in the bedroom."

Andy and Ashley were looking at each other and smiling. They also had big plans for later.

IQ got a call that his packages were on the way by special delivery drone. It contained a few surprises that he had rush ordered by calling from the hospital and were specially handmade from the expensive jewelry store in town that he always used. He signed for them and started to hand them out. The first one went to Ely. It was a bracelet made of the same expensive material as her locket. Letters were interlocking and spelled out "Team Badass" with the rest of the links being hearts. She was thrilled. The second went to Christy and was also "Team Badass," but the rest of the links were police badges, all gold shields, and the clasp was a tiny .45 which locked by pushing a pin down the barrel. The third went to Lea. It was "Team Badass" with links of nursing symbols and a clasp shaped like a stethoscope and heart. The fourth was a small box for Ben, and it held a ring made of tungsten with "Team Badass" engraved and in smaller letters, Bang on one end and Shock on the other. They all were overjoyed and thanked IQ over and over. It cost IQ a small fortune, but what was a life worth?

He asked everyone if lobster tails would be ok for supper and that he had asked Eva to join them if it was ok with his mom and dad. They said, "Of course she can."

He called Eva and sent his special drone to pick her up. He found out that his grandma and grandpa weren't coming. Grandma was feeling a little weak and just not herself, and IQ started to worry. Anything could happen at age 90. He talked to Ely, and they decided to go visit soon. He called his grandpa and thanked him for helping search for him. He said he loved them both.

IQ put in a massive order to be delivered in one hour. While everyone was talking and admiring the gifts, Christy pulled IQ aside, and she had just a couple of tears in her eyes. She said, "Darn you IQ, you know how I hate to cry. This is the nicest gift I ever received. It's perfect!"

"Sis, you saved my life and had my back more times than I could count. I love you."

"Aw dang, now you've done it," she said as she wiped her eyes. "I love you too!"

Ben came over and said, "IQ, this ring kicks ass, I love it! What material is it?"

IQ told him titanium was needed for a big manly guy, and they both laughed.

Lea said she absolutely loved her bracelet. IQ told her he could change the links if she decided to do something else with her life, but she would always be "Team Badass."

Ely wanted to sit on his lap and kiss away, but there were too many people around, and her Mom just landed in IQ's drone. It would have to wait. She noticed he was favoring his side and told him to sit for a while and rest. She would show her Mom in.

As Ely went out, IQ said, "Where are Stumpy and Sheba? I haven't even seen them since the big shoot out at the OK Corral."

Christy said, "They are sleeping off a big food coma. I made a huge pile of that chicken Sheba likes and had enough for Stumpy too."

"I have a new paw coming for Stumpy and wanted to tell him about it and also thank them both for helping save me. Sometimes I forget that they seem to understand everything we are talking about. It's uncanny."

Ely brought her mom in and everyone greeted her warmly, with Maria and IQ giving her hugs. She never had much of a family, and this warm greeting made her eyes wet. IQ said there were bonuses coming for all employees for coming in on the Priority 3 Lockdown and that she would be getting extra for dealing with all the annoying press. Eva pulled Ely aside later and told her to never let this one get away, as he was one in a million, kind, generous and loving. Ely said, "Don't worry Mom, he's my forever guy!"

The food drone arrival alert sounded, and IQ asked Ben, Andy and his Dad if they would bring in the food. His side was bothering him, and he had overworked today. It took two trips and what a feast it was. It cost a small fortune, but large drone sales were up and climbing. His miniaturized drones were being used by the FBI, CIA and many police departments. The police always had to watch out how they were used, as they had to get permission to record and surveil in many cases. As long as the sales went up, it was not his company's problem. Sales were through the roof, and he had exclusive manufacturing rights. If this next product they were working on could be perfected, he would be a multi-billionaire. He, Harold and Olive were very, very close to getting it working, but it might take another few months to work out all the bugs. This one had to be perfect, as lives would be at stake.

IQ excused himself before dessert and said he had to rest his eyes for a few minutes. He went into the enclosed lanai and fell fast asleep on a recliner. Ely was concerned and told the others that he was always working too hard, and she was worried about him. He seemed really tense, and it seemed to have something to do with the secret project he, Harold and Olive were working on. Ely went into the lanai and carefully put a cover over IQ and kissed his forehead. After dessert, the party broke up, and Ely and her Mom took IQ's drone to their house and sent it back empty to Microdots for automatic recharging, just like IQ had shown her. Maria and Danny let IQ sleep all night in the recliner, and he woke up in the morning refreshed and ready to go.

It was a Sunday, and he wanted to take a short walk with Ely and Stumpy. He also asked Christy if she wanted to go and take along Sheba. He said he needed to walk real slowly for a while. Ely rushed right over to his house as he was thanking and praising the two pets for helping save his life. They both were listening intently as he said he would get Sheba a brand new huge catnip doll and Stumpy a massive chew toy, as well as a new improved paw. He had reattached the damaged one, but told Stumpy the new one would be 10 times better. Sheba and Stumpy both tried a new happy dance, and IQ applauded and hugged them both. Danny was awake drinking coffee, and told him to look up in the sky and wave before he started out, as there would be a large black FBI drone keeping an eye on them from now on. There would be no repeat attempt at kidnapping. They got plenty of waves and hellos from neighbors, passing golf carts, bikers and walkers, all saying how glad they were to see all of them were OK. Sure enough, they saw the large black drone, as silent as a ghost, blink out a light when they waved. Police patrol EV's went past a couple of times, and they were amazed at the new level of security being provided for them. IQ, Ely and Christy discussed how they possibly took their safety for granted in the past. They would discuss better situational awareness with Ben and Lea when they saw them. It was what Grandpa Turner had told them about many times. Ely said she saw the drone, but she didn't give it much thought as she hurried over to his house. She had seen it approach closer to give her a look and then back off. She waved to it again and made a heart symbol with her hands. She got a double flash of the lights this time, and IQ laughingly said he was jealous. She clung to him as tight as a "tick on a hound dog," another of his grandpa's favorite sayings.

Maria and Danny were both drinking coffee and talking about last night. They talked about how generous and kind their boy was and how close they came to losing him.

Danny asked about Ely's angel remarks, and Maria made him promise not to tell anyone else, especially IQ. When she explained about the day IQ went over and introduced himself to Ely in the cafeteria, Danny was shocked. He said, "That poor child, maybe God did send an angel that day! I think they are made for each other."

Maria said, "I heartily agree, and there is something else she whispered to me and made me promise not to tell anyone, even you. Promise!"

"Maria, I can keep a secret better than anyone you know. What was it?"

"Her father would sneak into her bedroom at night and touch her inappropriately when she was just a child. When she finally told her Mom, he accused Ely of lying and slapped her around. That's when her Mom told him to get out and is probably why Eva doesn't trust men. I think she used to blame Ely too for the breakup, but she seems to be coming around now that she met IQ and our wonderful family.

She is an attractive woman, and I hope she finds someone as wonderful as you, Mr. Danny Turner.”

“Aw Maria, come here. That sweet girl deserves IQ after her childhood, and you deserve a whole bunch of love from me. That SOB husband of hers had better never show his face in this area again. I’m going to do a deep search on him tomorrow.”

Ely, IQ, Christy and the pets came in and caught them kissing and started teasing them.

Maria and Danny said, “Hey, we’re not that old yet! Heck, even your grandma and grandpa still kiss and hug.” They got the expected “nos and uggs” from the kids.

IQ asked if his grandma was ok and mentioned that she never says she is tired. She was always raring to go. He and Ely seemed really worried, so Maria decided to find out from grandpa soon. What she finally dragged out of grandpa was shocking. It was thought that Grandma Sunny had developed ALS, for which there was still no cure. Meds, diets and exercises could slow the progression, but life expectancy was only 2-5 years. When they told all the kids, Ely had the worst reaction. Sunny had always treated her as if she was her real grandchild, encouraged her and told her she was proud of her grades in school. Ely absolutely adored her, as she didn’t know her real grandparents well, especially on her father's side of the family.

Ely went to visit Grandma Sunny without telling IQ or anyone else in the family. When grandpa opened the door, she gave him a quick hug and ran to Grandma Sunny with tears in her eyes. She hugged her and started bawling her eyes out, saying, “I don’t want you to be sick, Grandma. I love you Grandma. It’s not fair. It’s just not fair!”

Sunny comforted her for a long time, holding her tight with her arms around her. Sunny explained that sometimes with old age things like this just happen, and you have to accept it, but you can still fight like Hell. “You just promise me that you’ll visit me, even when I get really bad.”

Ely said, “Grandma, I promise you.”

Sunny said, “You promise to take care of our IQ. He loves you so much and always tells me how wonderful you are.”

Ely said, “Grandma, he saved my life. I would never break his heart or hurt him in any way. I’m going to love him and keep him forever.”

Ely hugged her grandpa on the way out and said she loved them both. She said she would be back soon and bring IQ along next time.

Sunny and BD discussed how sweet and loving Ely was and the comment about IQ saving her life. They thought she helped save his life. Ely was true to her word and brought IQ over to visit weekly. IQ researched all the latest info on ALS in hopes of finding new cures and called several of the top researchers in the field, but to no avail. He vowed to donate more money into finding a cure.

On Monday, IQ decided to pick Ely up in his fancy large drone to go to school for his first day back. They touched down in the large courtyard near the entrance with many of the kids watching. IQ helped Ely down and pushed a button on his keyfob, closing the gull wing doors. The drone lifted off and headed back to Microdots. IQ had an amazing reception at school with kids and teachers alike cheering and greeting him. Ely was so happy for him and had gifted him in the drone with a copper, snap-on wristband. She had it made for him with "Team Badass" in script and with "Love Always From Ely" etched on it. It had taken all the money she had saved, but it was worth it to see his reaction. He wanted to fly right past the school and just keep kissing her, but he had to show up sometime. The whole "Team Badass" had worn their gifts, and their classmates were all admiring them. It took the teachers half of the class time to get everyone settled down. The girls were all checking out IQ's new looks and commenting to Ely how lucky she was to have a good looking millionaire for a boyfriend. She just smiled.

Chapter 19
Ely's Time In The Spotlight

Ben and Ely had been hitting a tennis ball around just for fun after school occasionally, and she was doing really well for someone who had never played before. She never broke a sweat and never seemed to get tired, even in the Florida heat. He taught her all the rules of the game, and she was really fast on the court with a vicious backhand. Ben mentioned to the coach how good she was getting and talked her into trying out for the team. IQ also encouraged her to try out, and if she didn't like it, well, no harm, no foul.

Ely made the team with ease, and the coach decided to try her out in a singles match against the next team they would be playing at their home courts. He didn't expect much from a beginner, but the team they were going up against was not too good. The team uniforms were halter type tops with very short pleated skirts and tight panties. Ely looked amazing in her outfit with her perfect build, tanned arms and legs and hair in a big ponytail. IQ made it a point to attend the match and couldn't stop staring at her.

"How in the world can we wait for over two more years?" he wondered. "She's perfect, just perfect!"

Ely made quick work of her opponent, 6-1, 6-1. She ran the poor girl ragged with her backhand, hitting from one side of the court to the other. Ely never broke a sweat and leaped over the net to hug the other girl after the set, making sure to compliment her for her good serves. Ely had to work on her own serves because of having to use that odd left hand to toss the ball into the air. The coach was astounded and quite pleased.

Ely couldn't wait to tell Maria and Danny about the match and dragged IQ to their home still wearing her tennis outfit. She was so excited, and between the kissing and chattering away, IQ couldn't get a word in. She ran into the house yelling, "Mama, Mama!"

She grabbed Maria and spun her around in a little dance, telling her all about it as IQ stared away. She was bouncing around and saw Danny out in the lanai.

She yelled out, "Papa, Papa" and went running out to show him how she used her backhand.

IQ called his Mom over and said, "Mom, I just can't, I just can't!"

He was rubbing his forehead and gesturing with both hands at Ely in her sexy little outfit. Maria knew what was on his mind and said, "Just use your best judgment and protection."

He said, "Mom, she doesn't even know the effect she has on guys. She seems so innocent. I love her so much and don't want to ruin anything, but just look."

Maria was smiling as Ely came back after hugging Danny. She hugged Maria again and asked IQ if they could go for a burger to celebrate.

IQ said, "Great idea, you could shower and change at Microdots while I talk to Harold and Olive."

Maria and Danny watched them as they left, and Danny said, "Wow, what a ball of fire and such a cutie! IQ will have his hands full with that girl."

Maria said, "Yes. and probably sooner rather than later." They smiled at each other.

Ely won every set and match except in the last match of the season. She went up against the top player in the state, and they were tied at one set apiece. Ely strung the last game of the final set out to 21 points and just missed a ball she had run all the way across the court to get. There were photographers there from several press agencies, and they got a picture of her lunging for the ball almost parallel to the ground with a determined look on her face. They used the shot in the newspaper and video on TV with the caption, "Ely Simmons takes State Champion to 3 sets and an amazing last game of 21 set points before almost making an impossible return! Even with the loss, she once again showed her incredible sportsmanship by leaping across the net and congratulating the winner with a smile on her face." Ely told the coach that she was sorry and had really tried to win.

The coach said, "Ely, you played wonderfully all season and helped get us to the district championship. I'm very proud of you!"

"Team badass" had all come to the match and congratulated her. Even Maria and Danny were there cheering her on. IQ noticed she was much quieter and not as upbeat afterwards, and he told her that he couldn't be prouder of her. He said the girl she played had been playing since she was 8 years old and had lessons from professionals.

Ely said, "Can we go somewhere quiet for dinner, just you and me? IQ, I don't like to lose."

He hugged her and said, "You will never lose me, and I would never criticize you for giving 100% like that."

She got back to her old cheerful self at dinner and sat on his lap kissing him all the way back to Microdots in the drone.

Ely had been observed by the coach of the cross country team, and he noticed that Ely never seemed to get tired. He had three runners out with the flu and decided to ask her to run in the next meet. She told him she had never tried to do a 5K, but she would try to help out the team. IQ took her shopping for the top pair of running shoes.

She said, "What do I do, is there a strategy involved?"

The coach just told her to cross the finish line first. He said to go out with the fastest runners on the other team and try to keep up and pass them at the finish line if she could. Ely not only won the race, but she crossed the finish line at least 100 yards ahead of everybody. She cheered on both teams and congratulated everyone in her usual display of good sportsmanship as they crossed the finish line. The coach was pleased and couldn't wait for the next meet where they would go up against the top runner in the district. IQ couldn't make it to that meet, but he told Ely that he could possibly watch it via the FBI drone. He would make contact with the drone and arrange to move it in much closer.

Ely was warming up at the next meet and stretching when the top runner from the other team came over to talk. She was a pretty girl named Faith, but she had a large red birthmark on her neck and running up the side of her cheek. She asked Ely if she ever got bullied about her hand, and Ely told her how bad it was when she was younger. She said she almost gave up, but then she met IQ. They became almost instant friends as they talked about things, and they exchanged cell phone numbers. They hugged and wished each other good luck. Ely's coach was frowning, as he considered that to be fraternizing with the enemy. When the race started, both girls went out very fast and were on the way to breaking the district record. Ely pulled into the lead by about 50 feet, and they both were several hundred yards ahead of the pack when, suddenly, Faith grabbed her hamstring and fell to the ground. Ely glanced back just a few yards from the finish line, turned around abruptly and ran back to Faith. She helped her up and with Faith's arm around her shoulder was able to hop across the finish line with her. The coach was furious, even though Ely crossed the line first and won the race.

He started screaming at her that she should have finished the race first and then gone back to help later. "You ended up helping that girl to second place and gaining them team points."

Ely was shocked and said, "But she is my new friend, and she was hurt."

The coach was still hollering at her and waving his arms around. He didn't notice the large, black drone swooping down almost silently behind him. In seconds two agents in all black had him by the arms and were dragging him to the drone. Ely went over to Faith with one of the ice packs that were kept near the finish in a cooler and held it on her hamstring. Faith had tears in her eyes and thanked her for helping her. The coach from the other team and all the other girls did the same.

The press happened to be there and got some great shots and video which went on the news. They titled it, "Miss Ely Simmons gives up a possible district record run to go back and help her main opponent who was injured. She is well known for her incredible displays of good sportsmanship in tennis and now in cross country racing. It's too bad the coach does not have the same ideals and is more interested in winning at all costs."

When the coach came back from the black drone, he had a chagrined look on his face with slumped shoulders. The men in black had given him quite a talking to about threatening gestures while screaming at the girlfriend of one of their key assets. They said he could disappear at any time, and they would be watching. Ely decided to give the black drone the heart symbol with her hands and got the double light blink in return.

She thought, "I bet IQ was watching the race." She wondered what he thought about her actions.

She didn't need to wonder when she got to her towel and belongings. Her phone had several messages, all heart shapes and gifs of hearts from IQ, saying, "You Rock, Miss Ely!"

Ely turned down all further requests to help the cross country team, but she stayed in touch with Faith, her new friend.

The coach made one more attempt to try to get Ely back on the team, but this time he corralled IQ outside of the school. The coach appeared to be arguing with IQ. "Team Badass" happened to see it going down and decided to intervene. This time they had no weapons available, so they decided to approach from three directions. Ben removed the handle from a mop left leaning against a cleaning trolley in the hallway. He made it look like he had a shock/bang stick in his hands. Christy and Lea approached from the other two sides. The black drone was swooping down at a rapid speed. The coach looked all around and quickly headed off in defeat. The gang had heard IQ talking really loudly and getting red in the face. This was a first, as they had never seen him get angry.

He had told the coach, "My wonderful girlfriend agreed to help your struggling team out of the goodness of her heart. She had no training and didn't even have the proper running shoes. Then she wins her first two races and gets screamed at by an asshole for showing compassion and good sportsmanship! What kind of coaching is that?"

This is when they and the drone appeared. IQ thanked the team and headed back into the school to have a long talk with the principal. The next day the coach was fired. Ely heard about everything from the team and was surprised and kind of thrilled that IQ actually got so angry and defended her so strongly. She decided on a course of action that she had been thinking about for a long time.

Chapter 20
Stress Relief

IQ was smiling as he read a handwritten thank you card from Albert Johnson, his top janitor. Albert had come to his office after hearing from Harold that IQ wanted to see him on the Monday after IQ was released from the hospital. Albert was more than a little apprehensive, because all his life he knew that being called in to see the boss never ended well. This time, however, was quite different. IQ greeted him warmly and had him sit down for some coffee. He gave him a few sheets of paper. Albert studied them and saw that it was a copy of his mortgage with a "paid in full" stamped on the front.

The title was in an attached envelope. He said, "Mr. IQ, I don't understand?"

IQ smiled and said, "Albert, you saved my life with your quick thinking, and no amount of money can ever repay that. I have something else I want to offer you."

He handed Albert a paper with a promotion to handle the extremely delicate cleaning operations in the Class 3 section, if he wanted it. It paid double what he was making, but he would need training with new equipment and it required wearing the "Clean Suits" used in that part of the building. He would also have to interview and train someone to take over his present job. Because of the very secret nature of the new job, he would be provided with a drone to and from work and tell no one what went on there.

Albert said, "Mr. IQ, I just can't thank you enough. I accept and promise to do an exceptional job."

IQ said, "I know you will and congratulations."

Albert left with a spring in his step and looked 20 years younger. If anyone ever said anything bad about his boss, he would be all over them.

Ely continued to worry about IQ being so stressed out and mentioned it a few times to Maria and to Grandma Sunny. She kept her promise to visit her grandma often, and this time grandma whispered some advice about how she used to "destress" grandpa when he came home from his job all worked up.

This advice had them both giggling, and Ely said, "Oh Gram, you're a pip!"

Gram called it canoodling, setting off another round of giggling.

Ely said, "I love you Grandma, I'll give it a try. I've been thinking about it for a long time."

"OK Ely, but use protection or name it after your grandpa or me!" More giggling!

Back at Microdots, Harold, Olive and IQ were having a meeting, and IQ was rubbing his forehead and turning his head side to side trying to relieve some stiffness.

"We have only a week to figure this last part out before the big presentation at the Pentagon. Word has it that the President himself may be there," said IQ, now pacing back and forth.

"Well, we know the main part of the design works flawlessly and the units themselves are perfectly reliable. We could specify that only bald people or short people could use them," said Harold.

Olive said, "I don't think that would be acceptable, since there are probably lots of females performing that line of work and some big CIA goons. Let's take a break and maybe something will come to us."

IQ was sitting in his office sketching some electrical designs, but no new ideas seemed to be popping into his head like they always did before. He put his head down into his hands and stared at the table hoping for some inspiration. Suddenly the door opened and Ely came in. He glanced up, and she was wearing the tiniest short skirt and tiniest halter top he had ever seen.

He said, "Oh Ely, I'm so sorry, I must have forgotten to call you, didn't I? We've been working like crazy."

Ely just stared at him with her big blue eyes and a just hint of a smile on her face.

IQ said, "Ely, is everything OK?"

She just nodded, reached back and blacked out the glass walls and locked the door.

"Ely, what's wrong? Did I do anything to hurt your feelings?"

Ely just shook her head no a little and continued to stare at him. Suddenly it dawned on him, "Was she giving me the 'cow eyes' that Daddy and Uncle Andy always joke about? Oh my God!"

Suddenly she reached behind her back and her top was off, and IQ stared at the most beautiful body he had ever seen.

"Ely? Are you sure?"

She nodded this time, and said softly, "Remember the panties comment?"

This time he could only nod.

She said, "Well, I'm not wearing any."

She walked over to him and with a flick of the wrist, dropped her skirt and pointed to the cot he used to catnap on. She led him over to the cot, and they didn't appear out of the office for over an hour.

Meanwhile Harold and Olive were wondering what was going on for them to blackout the office and deadbolt the door. They could hear lots of noises though and decided to go take a coffee break and maybe even tour the facility. Olive was pretty sure she knew what was going on and finally had to explain it to Harold. She wondered if they would ever get it on. She might need a little help from Ely. She knew Harold would stare at her and that he was very fond of her, but he seemed too scared to suggest anything.

When they got back to the office and the locked door finally opened, Ely came out with a smile and a very satisfied look on her face. Olive said, "Let me fix that tag hanging out of your top and your skirt is twisted. Your hair needs a little combing."

Ely said, "Harold, can you man the fort for a couple of hours? Olive and I are taking IQ's drone and going out."

He said, "Sure Ely."

Ely grabbed Olive's hand and said, "Come with me while I take a quick shower, and then we're going out shopping. I have spare clothing in my locker. We will have a nice talk."

Olive asked as they were walking, "Did you two do what I think you did?"

Ely said, "Yes, and God, it was wonderful! I think I relieved his stress. Don't tell anyone Olive, but it was our first time or many times, I should say! Olive, we tried everything!"

Ely was showered up and changed in record time. She put on a more demure outfit and looked fantastic. They got in the drone and headed for the beauty salon where Ely talked Olive into a new hairdo that better accentuated her face shape. Then they went clothes shopping. Olive had always worn some kind of shapeless outfit or pants, but Ely dressed her up in a skirt just above the knees and a sharp looking blouse. She turned her towards a full length mirror, and Olive was shocked. She actually looked really nice.

Ely said, "You need a couple more outfits to keep wowing Harold. You know he's in love with you, don't you?"

Olive said, "Yes, I'm pretty sure, but he won't make a move."

Ely said, "Here's what you do." She gave some great advice that Grandma Sunny told her and had Olive chuckling.

Olive said, "Tonight's as good a time as any. I'm going for it!"

"That's a girl," Ely said. "You got this."

While they were out of the office, IQ finally staggered out of his private office. Harold said that the girls had taken his drone out to go shopping. He said with a smile, "IQ old boy, your fly is half open, and your shirt is buttoned wrong." Harold started whistling a very old song by Buck Owens, "I've got a tiger by the tail, it's plain to see, I won't be much when you get through with me."

"Harold, what the hell just happened? My God, it was wonderful and amazing! In my wildest dreams, I never expected that it would be so good! I have to go take a shower."

IQ turned around and bumped into the trash can as he headed for the office. Harold could hear him mumbling, and it sounded like, "Insatiable, wonderful, amazing! She's insatiable!"

While IQ took a long shower, changed around and took a long coffee break, Olive returned and came walking into the office. Harold couldn't believe his eyes, she was beautiful. He was speechless.

Olive said, "Harold, your mouth is hanging open. Close it, go home, take a good shower and come to my place for supper. You will love what I have planned for dessert!"

Harold croaked out, "Olive, you're beautiful! I mean, you're even more beautiful! I would love to come for supper." He was wondering if what was for dessert was what he thought it was.

Smiling, Olive said, "Great, you might also get a little appetizer."

Harold hustled out of the office like a cat with its tail on fire.

Olive gave Ely a quick call and told her the plan was working like a charm.

Ely had IQ's drone leave her off at Mama T.'s house, but she hesitated outside for the longest time. They had promised to wait until they were 18 and graduated from school. She was worried that Mama T. would be mad at them. It so happened that Maria had seen the drone arrive, noted Ely's hesitation and pretty much surmised what had happened.

When Ely walked in, she went over to Maria and started to tear up. She said, "Mama, I have to tell you something. Please don't be mad at me!"

"Ely, I told you that you can always come to me and tell me anything. I think I already know. Did you use protection?"

"Yes Mama, and it was so wonderful," Ely said, while turning red and hardly able to look at Mama. "IQ is no longer all stressed out, that's for sure!"

"Ely, it's ok. When IQ saw you in your cute tennis outfit, he could hardly control himself. That's when I knew it would be soon. He loves you so much, just don't ever break each other's hearts."

"Mama, I love you, and I will love IQ forever! You're the best Mama ever!"

Ely hugged Maria for a long time, when suddenly a delivery drone showed up. Ely ran to the entrance and picked up a tiny package. The note attached said, "Dear Ely, I was saving this for your 16th birthday in a couple of days, but I wanted you to have it ahead of time. Love forever, IQ."

Ely showed Maria the package, and they opened it. It was a necklace made of interlocking tiny hearts with a tiny nude couple hugging all made of solid gold. It was beautiful and must have cost a small fortune.

Ely started to cry and told Maria, "IQ is always buying me such beautiful things, and I can't get him anything in return. I used all my allowance and savings on the copper bracelet I gave him."

Maria said, "IQ is not a guy who expects things in return. He has always given presents out of love. You know he wears that bracelet every single day."

Ely said, "Well then Mama, he is going to get lots of love in return!" She kissed and hugged Maria and headed out while texting and sending thank you and love notes to IQ.

The next day at Microdots, IQ, Harold and Olive all looked like different people. They were certainly more relaxed, and Harold and Olive couldn't stop looking at each other and smiling. Harold had brought in heart shaped donuts and Olive's favorite coffee. IQ knew something had happened, finally. He couldn't stop thinking about Ely. She was perfect, just perfect.

Suddenly Harold said, "A damn booster signal, just like WiFi boosters! Why it's so obvious. Let's use some kind of booster device and receiver."

Olive chimed in with her own idea. "Yes, a simple wired flesh colored patch, like a bandage. Put it on the forehead or temple or on a partially bald spot or even behind the ear. If there is a problem with height, we could slap one on the ankle."

IQ said, "It's Genius, why couldn't we see it. We were too stressed out. We can have them ready in days and just in time for the presentation."

They started to work on the idea immediately.

Chapter 21
The Rest of Team Badass

en and Christy were both honored with special awards, the Medal of Heroism and Medal of Lifesaving. Both of them were heartily congratulated by the entire police department at a special ceremony. They had brought Sheba and Stumpy along, and the two pets and the three police dogs, Chopper, Lance and Saber all received special pins. Sheba and Stumpy got Medal of Valor pins and Purple Heart Pins. The three police dogs got Commendation for Bravery Pins. All five saluted Top Police Chief, Josh Wilder, as he gave the awards out. He smiled and shook each paw. Even Sheba held hers out.

Stumpy said, "Sheba, we're heroes. Do you think there are any of those treats left in the office?"

"Oh my God, Stumpy, you won't starve to death until we get home."

"But Vickie, I've got a hollow leg, get it?"

Even Vickie had to laugh at that bad joke.

At the hospital where Ashley worked and Lea interned, a special award was given to Lea for her life saving efforts. She received a plaque and a specially made pin with the Medical Caduceus symbol and Lifesaver engraved on it. She was highly praised for her quick thinking efforts at the cabin. Ashley was beaming as she pinned it on her daughter.

After all the kidnapping commotion died down and the news reports turned to some other catastrophe or world disaster, Stumpy and Sheba were getting a little bored with the same old routine. But one morning, Ashley and Lea showed up at Maria and Dannys' house with their nursing outfits on. Only Christy was at home and was getting ready to go out shopping, so they asked if she thought Stumpy could go along to the Children's Rehab Center. They had a couple of patients with disabling injuries and thought if they showed them how good Stumpy was doing, it might cheer them up.

Christy said, "Sure, and why not take Sheba along. Kids love cats and dogs. They both are clean and did their duty outside this morning, so let's ask them."

They both nodded yes and actually did the little happy dance.

Christy said, "Now listen you two. Stumpy, you are much bigger and heavier than any of those kids, so be on your best behavior. Sheba, be very gentle please. You are bigger than any cat they have ever seen and no claws on the furniture or equipment or the kids."

Both nodded yes.

"Vickie, do you think they will have treats there?"

"Jim, you're killing me! You just had breakfast."

Ashley and Lea took them by EV Van. They had their new award pins on their collars and made quite an impression on the whole gang of kids. Everyone had heard of the big kidnapping and rescue. Lea explained about Stumpy's foot and how it was replaced after getting shot off by the kidnappers. He did the little happy dance for them to show how good it worked. Lea told the kids how brave they both were and how Sheba jumped from way up in a big tree to attack the biggest man with her sharp teeth and claws. She showed them the scar where the big guy had shot Sheba on her back. She told Sheba to show them her claws, and Sheba raised both front paws and extended her claws, getting ohs and ahs from the kids. She explained that cats whose owners declaw them suffer, because it's like getting your own fingernails pulled out. Every kid wanted to pet them both, and they gave their best efforts at rehab because Stumpy and Sheba watched and joined in on some of the exercises. Ashley gave Lea a big hug and said she did a great job with the kids. She told her that both she and her dad were very proud of her and Ben.

On the way home, Ashley said to Sheba and Stumpy, "You were so good with the kids. How about we stop at The Pet Palace and get some of that ice cream especially made for pets?" There was enthusiastic meowing and barking.

"Yes, I'm starving Vickie. That was really fun."

"When aren't you? You must be 250#, but I have to admit, it looks like mostly muscle."

Ashley and Lea decided to take them regularly to work with the kids.

Ely was doing errands at Microdots when she got a call from Ben. He asked about the cute, and well built runner he saw in the news that Ely had helped. She told him her name was Faith Roberts, and she was such a sweet girl. Ben asked for her number and told Ely he wanted to ask her out on a date.

Ely said, "Now listen Mr. Stud, she has never had a date because of her birthmark, and if you break her heart, I'll never forgive you. We became good friends, and we talk a lot."

Ben said, "That birthmark doesn't bother me, it's how nice a person is and how they treat others that I look for. Besides, she has a pretty face and a great build. I've got a great idea. How about we double date with you and IQ? Then you can keep an eye on me."

Faith was picked up by IQ's huge 4 passenger limo drone at her parents house. They were highly impressed when both Ben and IQ hopped out and introduced themselves. Ben gave them his cell phone # and address. He told them exactly where they were going and what time he expected to bring Faith home. He also told them his father was Lieutenant Anderson and to contact him if there were any problems. When Faith came out, she was dressed in a beautiful outfit with her hair all done up in the latest style.

Ben said, "Wow, you look amazing, Faith!" Ben held out his hand to assist her into the drone.

Ely got out and greeted Faith's parents, both of whom she had met before. They loved Ely for being so kind to their daughter and for helping her at the race. When they all had taken off in the drone, the parents looked at each other and commented about how nice those boys were and that Faith appeared to be in good hands.

Faith and Ely talked the next day about the fun date and how Ben had kissed her on the way to the front door. It was her first kiss from a boy, and she said he had asked her out again. She was so happy and Ely was happy for her. As it turned out, Ben and Faith became a steady couple.

Christy's pizza date with big Joe went very well. She asked him not to discuss the kidnapping, as she was still having nightmares. So they talked about school, football and future plans. It went very well and quite a few kisses were exchanged. It seems that big Joe was not just a dumb jock, but he intended to study criminology in college if he got in on a football scholarship. He thought she would make an outstanding police officer.

Lea was not into dating much yet, but she was so attractive that she could get any guy she wanted. She was busy studying all she could about nursing and was interested in pediatric care. She just loved working with children, taking after her mom and Grandma Sunny.

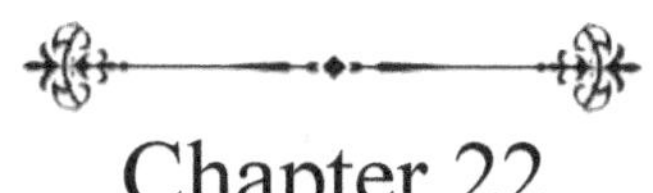

Chapter 22
The Making of a Billionaire

IQ, Harold and Olive were now in the testing stages of the top secret project and only days away from their meeting at the Pentagon. It was confirmed that the President would be attending. The testing was held in the Class 3 section in a sealed room away from the production area with electronic protection and monitoring, both video and voice. IQ had a couple of the production models in his hand, and they were very heavy, about the size of a deck of cards, but about 2" thick.

He gave one to Olive and asked her to try it out, saying, "Ladies first."

She said that because she was fairly tall, she might need a booster patch, but she would try it out first without one. The only control on it was a small on/off push button.

She said, "Here I go!"

Suddenly Olive disappeared, and Harold and IQ started applauding and yelling, "It works even without the booster patches."

All of a sudden, Harold was getting kissed and he jumped back, startled. Olive pushed the button and reappeared like magic, laughing with delight. "Why Harold, are you getting shy?"

A lot of high fives and back slapping were going on. They tested the time limit of the extremely dense and powerful solid state battery needed to run the device and found it to be one hour, exactly as their calculations predicted. They already knew about the construction and how it couldn't be defeated or copied. IQ wondered how many units they should take to the meeting. It cost a tremendous amount of money to produce the devices. They were almost at the limits of miniaturization due to the incredibly complex machinery needed. Even the case needed to be impenetrable when finished, or if penetrated, the battery and complex wiring would self-destruct. He decided to take three units out of the small batch of 10 they had in stock. All units were triple locked in a safe immediately after production.

IQ looked at Harold and Olive and asked them to dress sharply for the Pentagon meeting. They said almost in unisom, "You want us to go along?"

IQ said, "Yes, and if this goes as predicted and we can get the price I will be asking, I'm making you partners in Microdots, and it will be at 5% each. There are only a few other people in the world that I trust as much as you two."

Olive started crying, and even Harold had tears in his eyes. They told him that they loved working for him and were very grateful. He could count on them for anything at any time.

IQ told them that he would be bringing his dad along in full dress uniform and that he would get top secret clearance for everyone as well as FBI close support.

They were scheduled for Monday, and a top secret, long range FBI drone would pick them up at Microdots at 8AM sharp.

Sunday dinner at the Turner house was quite different than normal. Everyone knew about the Monday meeting, but only Danny and IQ knew what it was about. Ely came over after dinner and noticed IQ was unusually quiet and a little tense. IQ was sitting in a big recliner in the lanai talking to his Dad when Ely walked in. He motioned her over and told her about the meeting, but no particulars. He said that the less people that knew about it, the safer it would be. His Dad got up and went out to the kitchen to help Maria with the cleanup. When Maria peeked in the lanai, she saw Ely curled up on IQ's lap with her head on his chest. He would brush her hair back and kiss her forehead and she would sigh and smile. Maria was one happy mama. She saw that Christy had come back from outside and called her over to take a peek.

Christy said, "They were made for each other, Mom."

Mom hugged her and said, "I know I spent a lot of time with Ely, but she had a rough start in life. I love you so much and am so proud of you and don't want you to ever think I was favoring one over the other."

Christy said, "I know all about what happened to her and even why she calls IQ her angel. She told Ben, Lea and I, but not IQ. I know you love me Mom, and I wouldn't want any other mom in the world." Mom hugged her even tighter with tears in her eyes.

On Monday, IQ took off from school after a quick call to the principal. He and his Dad, who looked sharp in his dress uniform with the chest full of awards, left in IQ's drone for Microdots. Harold in a suit and Olive in a sharp looking outfit were already there. IQ also wore a suit. The three hustled upstairs, got out three devices and took 6 patches just in case. They were put in a locked briefcase. The long range FBI drone was huge and spacious inside. They got in and settled down for what they thought would be a long, boring trip. To their surprise, the drone converted in mid air to a high speed aircraft capable of 600 mph, and the trip went quickly. They discussed how to present the device, and Olive was picked for the demonstration. Captain Turner would go over the pros and cons of the device and its very possible dangerous misuse. Harold would go over the extremely difficult production and the expensive equipment needed to manufacture the device to perfect specs each time. IQ would present the cost/unit, knowing full well that the CIA and FBI would drool at the prospect of using them. IQ knew that if the presentation went well, he had them by the "shorthairs," so to speak.

IQ handed out plastic American flag lapel pins to wear for the meeting. The current president was an "America first" type of guy and would love to see the display. When the drone landed near the Pentagon there was a contingent of well armed FBI agents and a second outer ring of the Capitol Police already in position. IQ had warned them ahead of time about a very sensitive project that would be brought along. They were greeted by General Millworth who had worked with IQ on his first two projects, the horsefly sized spy drone and the smaller housefly sized drone. General Millworth now was on the Joint Chiefs of Staff and would be joining them. As they headed for the secure meeting room, he asked if IQ and his team could make the housefly, nicknamed "Buzz," any smaller. IQ said yes, but he explained how difficult it was to manufacture and how the smaller and lighter models were subject to being blown off course by even the slightest breeze. They were also near the limits of present battery design miniaturization. They had even lost one to an anole lizard while testing on the roof of Microdots. The lizard viewed it as an easy lunch when they went to land "Buzz Junior"! IQ promised to get back to him, as Harold was secretly working on a completely different idea using "Buzz," which wasn't quite ready.

When they entered the secure room, agents had just finished sweeping the room for bugs, and they announced that the President was on the way. They were introduced around the room to heads of the various agencies, with some looking at 16 year old IQ a little skeptically. They had heard reports and watched many videos of the kidnapping and were impressed by the security being granted to IQ and his "Team Badass" down in Florida, so he must have something going for him. They knew he was in the genius category.

President Miles Sanders entered the room surrounded by agents. He dismissed them all and said he would be quite safe here. He would not feel so secure ever again after he saw the presentation. IQ introduced his group, and the president greeted each one personally. He already knew about IQ's Dad and his good work in Florida. He glanced approvingly at the flag pins and nodded, just as IQ predicted.

IQ said, "We will start with the demonstration first before the explanation, as it will be quite dramatic."

He unlocked the small briefcase under the close watch of the FBI and CIA. He handed Olive one of the devices that they nicknamed "Grey Ghost" while flying to the meeting. He told them the nickname and said, "Watch Olive."

Suddenly, she disappeared and everyone's mouths were hanging open except IQ's group. The others were looking around the room and saying "No Way!" and "What the Hell just happened?" About 20 seconds later Olive appeared in the same location she had started in.

The President said, "Oh my God IQ, that's incredible," and everyone else was trying to ask questions at once.

IQ said, "Mr. President, would you turn around 180 degrees please?"

When he turned around there was a sticky note on the back of his coat with a sketch of a knife with drops of blood dripping off of it. "Damn and Holy Shit" were just a few of the phrases uttered by everyone in the room except the President, who pulled out a chair and sat down staring at the note. He immediately understood the significance of the "Grey Ghost" device.

IQ said, "My Father, Captain Turner, will now go over a few things, both pros and cons."

Danny said, "I'm sure you can see immediately some of the cons if this fell into the wrong hands. We are lucky that Miss Olive is a wonderful patriot, or she could have taken the whole room out one by one if armed with just a knife. That is con number 1. Con number 2 would be, anyone with this device could slip into any meeting discussing sensitive information, be it military or political, foreign or domestic. Can you imagine a double agent getting his hands on a 'Grey Ghost.' Assassinations could become a relatively simple thing."

"Some Pros would be, number 1, if our side used the 'Grey Ghost' to protect the United States by gleaning sensitive information from our adversaries. Number 2, it would be of great use to police forces to stop hostage situations, domestic violence calls and a whole host of other uses. Number 3, General Millworth, I'm sure, is thinking of a whole company of soldiers equipped with these devices and slipping behind enemy lines."

"These are just a few of the many things we discussed on the way here. Just for the record, I'm against using or selling this device, but it's IQ's call, and I trust him implicitly."

IQ glanced around and saw the heads of the FBI and the CIA looking at each other and nodding. He knew they badly wanted these devices.

IQ said, "Now everyone, Harold will discuss a few things about the device you absolutely must be made aware of."

Harold was given the device by Olive who smiled at him and winked. He said, "Number 1, a 'Grey Ghost' can be switched on and off numerous times, but the life span is only one total hour of use. It uses enormous amounts of battery power, and you can tell that by its heavy weight. The battery is the most compact, solid state, powerful battery ever produced, and we manufacture it at Microdots.

"Number 2, it can not be opened, cut into or drilled into. It can not be accessed through the small push button. If any of these methods are tried, it will self-destruct. It can not be X-Rayed, put into an MRI unit or any other type of invasive technique.

"Number 3, the user must keep accurate time of exactly how long it's been in operation.

"Number 4, if it's put down somewhere while turned on, it will be invisible, so it must be in your possession at all times. It will self-destruct on its own in exactly one hour. Now we know the military has been experimenting for many years with 'cloaking type devices,' but this is entirely new technology, and we want each of you to try it for yourself."

Harold pushed the button and was gone from sight. There were more "Damns and Holy Craps" uttered. He appeared back into view on the other side of IQ who handed it to his Dad with the same results. Everyone tried it out, and IQ had put his small folding computer on mirror mode so they could attempt to see themselves. The President was immensely impressed, as were the rest of the group. When he handed the device back to IQ, he turned it on and laid it in an ashtray.

IQ said, "There is about a half hour to go, and we want you to see what will happen at the one hour mark. See how easily it can be misplaced."

"We have a proposal and conditions for you to look at gentlemen while we are waiting. We will scrap the project altogether if these are not agreed to. We are all patriots at our company and 100% loyal to the USA. If you are worried about the technology falling into the wrong hands, I assure you it will not. We also have a robust security system set up at Microdots.

"Number 1, we will be the sole manufacturer and supplier!

"Number 2, we have vetted every single employee, and I think you will find them incorruptible! We want them all protected. If any are missing, killed or harmed in any way, we shut the program down. This applies to my entire family, my girlfriend Elyssia Simmons and even our two pets.

"Number 3, if we notice any unusual unexplainable harm of any type, assassinations or attempted assassinations anywhere in the world, we will shut the program down until a reasonable and verifiable cause is found.

"Number 4, the cost is so extremely high to produce these, and the assembly technology is so difficult, that we must ask for what may seem to be an extraordinarily high price of $500,000,000 per unit.

"As General Millworth knows from our past dealings, our technology has been extremely reliable, and we are working on another project or two for him which could be ready in one or two years. We think they will come in quite handy for the CIA and FBI.

"Mr. President, if you want to discuss the terms with us out of the room, it's perfectly fine. Do you have a coffee break room closeby?"

The President called for two agents to escort them and their briefcase to a breakroom. Soon after they left, the device in the ashtray started smoking and burst into flame, melting into a mass of useless material. It was exactly at the one hour mark of usage.

The meeting was very short with everyone agreeing that this kid and his team were brilliant, and the units were well worth the exorbitant price! They were called back into the room and the terms sheet and a contract for 25 "Grey Ghost" units was signed.

IQ said, "Gentlemen, we are giving one unit to you as a symbol of good faith, as well as two units of what we call, 'Grey Ghost Boosters.' If you have an agent of over 6' 4" in height, he or she may need to put on a patch behind the ear or on the neck and possibly one on the ankle depending on where the main unit is carried. These also self-destruct in one hour when activated by the main unit or if an attempt is made to open one. We will get production started immediately on return to Microdots and notify General Millworth when the units are ready, or we can deliver any part of the order on your say-so as soon as they are produced. Use the spare unit to test out on your tall agents, and any 'Boosters' you need in the future will be free. It seems as if you may not need any, but test just in case. Mr. President, it was an absolute honor to meet you. We brought along a parting gift for you that you may want to consider using at any high risk events. It's a full body 'Invisa-Shield' weighing next to nothing. We took your measurements from videos and photos of you and our computers designed it especially for you."

President Sanders said, "IQ, thank you and your team for your patriotism to the USA, and it was our pleasure to meet you all."

IQ, Harold, Olive and Danny were all ushered back into another high speed drone, and it took off with IQ motioning to not talk. He thought that there might be voice recordings and or video in the drone. A quick search found there were not and the high fives and hugging started. Harold got a couple of Olive's kisses, and IQ suddenly missed Ely tremendously. His Dad told him how immensely proud of him he was and hugged him a couple of times. IQ said not to discuss the terms of the contract until they arrived back at Microdots. He told Harold and Olive that they were now each 5 % owners and partners in Microdots. They could sign the paperwork tomorrow. They both almost broke down and thanked him over and over. IQ called Ely and told her the good news. She told him she couldn't wait to see him. He asked if she could possibly wear what she wore that day she came into his office, and she burst out laughing and told him, "Of course."

Danny called Maria and told her their son was amazing and gave a fantastic presentation. He spoke about meeting the President and would tell her later about everything.

Ely called for IQ's private large drone and rode back to Microdots with her tiny outfit on, sans underwear. When they returned, she called him over and as the others went home, she had the drone hover above Microdots while they used the backseat. IQ hoped the battery was well charged, as Ely was raring to go. He never enjoyed himself so much and told her he couldn't wait until they were married and had a house to themselves. They told each other over and over how much they loved each other. They finally landed and were all worn out. Ely said she better shower and change out of her "hooker outfit" that her Mom had never even seen. He laughed and said maybe he could join her in the shower. Well, that consumed another half hour. He dropped her off at her house with a kiss and finally headed home. When he got in the door, Mom, Dad and Christy all smiled and said he looked really tired. They knew what he had been up to. His Dad had seen them go up in the drone and just hover. His Dad had not mentioned the contract, so IQ told them the company was now worth over $12,500,000,000 plus the rest of the many millions it was already bringing in.

Christy said, "Holy Shit IQ, and you met the President!" Mom was speechless and just hugged him tightly.

The next day at school he was asked about a hundred times how meeting the President was. He told them that he was a real gentleman, intelligent and very polite. He told them about flying in the high speed FBI drone and meeting stern looking CIA and FBI agents. He told everyone that the reason for the meeting was top secret and couldn't be discussed. The kids were highly impressed and between that and the kidnapping, IQ was becoming a sort of folk hero.

Later that afternoon IQ had a meeting with Harold and Olive and officially made them Junior Partners in Microdots. He called a mandatory meeting with all employees. Many were worried that the company might be in financial trouble. When IQ announced that a major government contract had been signed and everyone would be getting a substantial bonus, there was wild cheering and clapping. He also announced a major expansion due to the continued growth of the large drone segment. He introduced Harold and Olive as Junior Partners, and it was well received by all. IQ said there would be space allocated in the new expansion project for a large day care center, and it would be at no cost to the employees. It would be staffed with qualified staff and a nurse. He thanked everyone for their hard work and told them that they may see some unusual surveillance drones and/ or personnel in or around the building or even watching them outside of work to guarantee their safety. This was due to the new government contact which he could not discuss.

He, Olive and Harold discussed the possibility of the CIA or FBI testing the security of the building and particularly the Class 3 section. Olive said she had been thinking they might even sacrifice one of the "Grey Ghost" devices just to see if the security was as good as IQ promised. She came up with the idea of simple weight recording mats with a silent alarm system sending an alert to security. They might be invisible, but they wouldn't be weightless.

IQ and Harold said it was a fantastic and inexpensive idea. They started on implementing it that day. All entrance doors and the entrance door to Class 3 had the mats installed, and they tested them out. It was impossible to enter the building even from the roof entrance without applying weight to a mat. They would use a simple camera system so that regular traffic across the mat would be seen by the cameras and matched to the weight first and not send an alarm. It worked perfectly, and IQ crawled across one mat under the cameras and set the alarm off for a test run of an invisible person. They then adjusted the cameras to compensate for all heights. The security guard dogs would then sniff out the intruder. Another security concern was if a mini-drone similar to Microdots' "Buzz" would fly in while doors were opened. IQ solved that problem by installing air blast systems at all doors to be activated when the doors were first cracked open. They were tested by attempting to fly a "Buzz" model inside against the strong breeze. It was blown far away. The air blasts were not popular with the Ladies whose hairdos were affected, but they understood the necessity.

As it turned out, nobody from the government ever came to test out the security of the building. They either believed IQ's claim of excellent security or didn't want to waste a very expensive "Grey Ghost" unit.

Only one employee was ever approached about getting into the building or getting sensitive information. He was offered a very substantial bribe when he was heading for home after work. It was a big mistake, because it happened to be Albert Johnson. It took him all of 5 seconds to tell them to go to Hell. He said nobody at Microdots would betray IQ for any amount of money. He made an immediate call to IQ to inform him about the bribe offer and his reply. IQ thanked him profusely.

Chapter 23
Two Great Years

The Junior and Senior years seemed to fly by with "Team Badass" easily holding the top 5 positions academically. Ely continued to play tennis very successfully, winning nearly every match. She was coaxed back onto the cross country team by the new coach, this time a woman who loved her team spirit and good sportsmanship. She won nearly every meet, posting several school records. Ely had made many friends from other schools, but her favorite was Faith, whom Ben was still dating. They got along famously, and it looked to Ely like they were getting serious. She was always telling Ben, "Don't you dare break my best friend's heart!"

Christy and big Joe were still an item, and he was getting some serious looks from various colleges and a possible football scholarship. Both Ben and Christy planned to attend the Police Academy immediately after graduation.

Lea still hadn't found "The One", but she was working in the new daycare center for IQ as well as interning, and the kids adored her. Stumpy and Sheba would go almost every day to help out. The children all loved them.

IQ's company was doing spectacularly, and with Ely's new, "Relaxation Therapy", as she laughingly referred to it, new ideas were coming fast and furious.

Ely's Mom, Eva, was finding various small gifts on her office desk almost daily, and she thought maybe it was IQ or Ely. There were small boxes of her favorite candy, pastries or coffee still hot when she arrived. She called up Ely and IQ to thank them, but they said they weren't doing it. Ely teased her and said she had a secret admirer. Eva was stumped. This had never happened to her, and she wondered who it might be. It felt really nice, and she was determined to find out who it was. She came in very early one day and finally caught him in the act. It was the quality control chief, Manny, a handsome guy who had lost his wife to a car accident a couple of years ago. He was five years older than Eva and told her he was scared to ask her out. He said his wife was the only girl he had ever dated and that Eva looked very much like her.

Eva said, "Ask me to go out."

On their first date, he took her to her favorite restaurant. She had never been treated so nicely in her life, and they became a steady couple after that.

Harold and Olive got engaged, much to IQ's delight. It seemed to IQ that Ely had leaked her "Relaxation Therapy" technique to Olive, because Harold was coming up with great ideas right and left.

IQ had accumulated so much wealth that he decided to start a 2 billion dollar philanthropy organization. He would approach Ely to see if she would head the organization. He knew she would be perfect, as she was very smart, compassionate, and could direct any money to the people or organizations that needed it the most. He would call it the Turner Foundation. He approached Ely on the subject, and she was shocked that he considered her to run it. He said they would use only income from the invested money and not touch the initial amount. He would add to it as conditions with the company warranted. She could have secretaries and a large office at Microdots, and they could see each other more often. He would pay her a generous salary with benefits, of course. Ely hesitated for a few seconds and told him yes, she would do it.

IQ had secretly purchased an acoustic Martin Guitar customized with pearl inlays saying 'Ely and IQ Forever.' It was a work of art costing over $100,000. He learned to play on his own and was getting pretty good when Ely stumbled in on him one day practicing and singing. He was a little embarrassed, but Ely loved it. She started to sing along, and he was amazed at her beautiful voice. They both loved grandma and grandpas' old 1950's and 1960's music where you could actually hear the words and nice melodies, not the mumbo jumbo techno electronic songs that were out in this day and age.

He asked her to sing a song at the annual senior talent show, and he would also. They could share the stage, and he would play for her. It took a whole lot of convincing. She was scared of appearing in front of a whole auditorium with friends and even family watching. He said he was going to do an Elvis Prestly song. She said she would consult with grandma and tell him later. He told her to give him a few days to practice and make it sweet and easy. IQ picked, "Love me Tender" from 1956, over 130 years earlier. He wasn't even sure the kids of today had even heard of Elvis, but it was a beautiful song and fairly easy to play. Ely came back to him and told him she had picked, "I Love How You Love Me," by the Paris sisters from 1961.

Grandpa had played it for her and had given her the lyrics and a copy of the song. It took them a full week until they felt comfortable with the two songs. When the class heard they were entered, everybody wanted to come. Ely's mom and the whole Turner family were there. It was a full auditorium. Grandma and Grandpa were put down front, as Grandma Sunny now needed a wheelchair. There were several acts ahead of them that were only just ok, and then suddenly they were on the stage. Ely was just about scared to death, and IQ said he would go first and to just watch him and listen to the lyrics. The kids in the class had their cell phones out and were video recording IQ's song and when it ended with "For My Darling, I Love You, and I Always Will," they saw a tear roll down Ely's eye and her hand go over her heart. There was a huge applause including grandpa, and even Grandma Sunny tried to applaud a little bit. When it got quiet, up came the cell phones again, and Ely almost froze.

She whispered to IQ, "I don't think I can do it."

He said, "Just look at me, and sing it just to me." He turned his stool toward her and she did the same toward him.

She sang beautifully, and when she ended with, "I love how you squeeze me, tease me, please me, I love how you love me, I love how you love me, I love how you love me." She whispered, "I love you IQ."

The mike picked it up and also IQ saying back, "I love you Ely."

There was dead silence in the auditorium for a couple of seconds until grandpa stood up and started to applaud, and then Ely got a standing ovation. She started crying and hugged IQ. They waved and left the stage. It was no contest. Ely and IQ won by a landslide, and kids in school the next day were listening to their songs on their phones and through earbuds. IQ and Ely took the drone up for a long hover that night.

Graduation was fast approaching, and IQ had big plans. He asked the principal if he could do a drone show and that his speech as Valedictorian may be a little different than usual. Of course he got the OK. After the usual speeches, IQ was called up and announced as Valedictorian with the highest ever recorded grades. He said that his speech would be a little different. He said he would not be attending college, as he already had a line of work to pursue. There was a lot of laughter, as everyone knew he was a billionaire. IQ congratulated everyone in the class and thanked all his teachers for letting him study independently.

Then he told them, "You do not have to attend college as long as you pursue a passion. There is no such thing as a bad job if you like what you are doing. There was a vast need for skilled labor in all kinds of fields, electrical, air conditioning, plumbing, construction and heavy equipment operation. If you want to pursue any of these jobs, do it with a passion and learn as much as you can about the job. Go to a trade school or community college, or be an intern somewhere. Just be the best in your field, and you will be in high demand.

"When your AC fails, and it will, you will want the best trained person you can find. I would like to introduce you to someone that I invited here. His name is Albert Johnson, and he works for me. I also consider him as a good friend. What's his job? He started as a janitor and is now in charge of what we call the 'Class 3 Clean Room' where only the highest trained people are allowed to enter. He does a wonderful job and has gotten raise after raise. That's what I mean by doing something with a passion. This happens to be the same gentleman who helped save my life. While recovering from Covid, he sent up his personal drone, located where I was being held and directed my 'Team Badass' to the location to save me. Albert, please stand."

Albert got a standing ovation.

"I have just a couple more announcements. Miss Elyssia Simmons, could you come up here please?"

She walked up, but didn't know why. IQ said, "There is a new award this year that will be an annual thing. This is a little different, as it is voted on by all of the schools in the whole district. We have a young lady from Ellington High School to present the award. This is Miss Faith Roberts."

Faith came up with a large plaque and said, "The new yearly award is called 'The Good Sportsmanship Award' and covers all sports. Elyssia Simmons was picked by unanimous decision for this award." She handed it to Ely and gave her a hug. She whispered, "I love you Ely."

Ely was speechless. She got a lot of applause from both the class and from the audience.

IQ said, "Ely, stay right here for a few minutes. Sorry folks, but just a few more minutes please. My company, Microdots, has started a philanthropy organization called The Turner Foundation, and Miss Elyssia Simmons will be heading it up. We have decided to pay the first year bill of every 2086 class member who attends college, community college, trade school, nursing school, or any other type of training requiring money. You will provide the paid bill and type of training, and you will be reimbursed by the foundation. Remember, pursue it with a passion to be the best."

There was thunderous applause this time. "Now we have a little extra to show you."

Suddenly a massive drone display lit up the sky with "Congratulations Class of 2086" and simulated a display of fireworks, the school mascot charging across the sky and at the end spelling out in huge cursive letters, "Miss Ely, will you marry me?" The drones turned into a huge red heart with one lighted drone heading for the stage carrying a small package right towards Ely. She was crying when she opened it and saw a beautiful engagement ring with a heart shaped diamond flanked by smaller heart shaped diamonds. It was gorgeous, and IQ took it and got down on one knee.

She said, "Yes! Yes! Yes!" and pulled him up for a kiss.

The whole place erupted with cheers as he put the ring on her right ring finger. Maria, Danny, Andy, Ashley and Eva were in the audience, and Maria was bawling like a baby. Danny said, "Maria, you should be happy."

She said, "I am."

Eva was also crying, but was very happy for her daughter. Ely and IQ were getting congratulations from just about every one of their classmates, teachers and family. It took a long time until they had the big drone to themselves. Ely was wearing only her engagement ring and IQ only his copper wristband on the way to his parents house for a big graduation party. Everyone had a hunch about why it took them so long to arrive.

Chapter 24
Wedding Bells

Ely and IQ discussed when and where they would hold their wedding, who and how many people to invite and who to get to officiate. They decided against a big church wedding. While they believed in a higher power, they preferred to hold hands and pray together. IQ said that his grandpa was a wedding officiant and may agree to perform the ceremony. He was thrilled when they asked him. They decided to keep it short and sweet and would write their own vows. They decided to use the very large meeting room at Microdots. It was large enough to hold over 300 people, and they came up with a great plan to decorate the mostly bare space. Small, long range silent drones would hover with streamers of flowers hanging down from ceiling to floor. It would require quite a few, with several hours of run time, and Olive and Harold were put in charge of programming them and overseeing the decorations. Tables and chairs would be set up and decorated by the "Team Badass" crew. They arranged catering of food from Ricardo's and decided on old time entertainment from back in the 1950's and on up to 2023, that they knew grandma and grandpa would love.

When IQ and Ely were at Danny and Maria's for dinner one evening, Ely saw Danny alone out in the lanai staring out the window at yet another approaching thunderstorm. She went out and said, "Papa, can I ask you for a favor?"

He said, "Sure, Ely."

Ely took his hand and said, "Papa, would you walk me down the aisle and give me away?"

It was the first time anyone ever saw tears in Danny's eyes, and he said, "Ely, that is a huge honor, and nothing would give me greater pleasure."

Ely gave him a kiss and a hug and ran out to tell IQ.

Maria walked out and saw him rubbing his eyes, and teasingly said, "Why you big softy, come here to Mama T."

She gave him a big hug and a kiss. He said, "That girl is so sweet. I'm so happy for IQ."

Maria said, "I can't wait to hold some grandkids."

Ely and IQ asked Stumpy and Sheba to come over to them. They told them about the wedding and asked if they would be ring bearers together with Sheba carrying one and Stumpy the other. There was enthusiastic head nodding and a couple of happy dances. They decided on a very small wedding but a huge reception. They would invite the entire Microdots staff to the reception including significant others. Ely asked her best friend, Faith, to be her Maid of Honor, and she was thrilled. She asked Lea, Christy and Olive to be Bridesmaids. IQ asked Ben to be his Best Man and Harold and Big Joe to be groomsmen. He talked to Lea about whether she had a hidden significant other he could ask to be a groomsman so that everyone in the wedding would be matched up perfectly.

Lea said, "Well, there is one nice guy I've been kind of seeing, but he's 25 years old, and I don't want to give daddy a heart attack. He's an EMT and handsome."

IQ said, "Let's ask him. I'd like to meet him."

It turned out that her guy, Phil Williams, was really a nice guy and a big fan of Microdots. He was happy to be asked to participate.

So everything was set but security. IQ called his FBI contact and told him what to expect. They would supply several more close support drones, and they suggested simple wristbands for the reception that could be scanned at the entrance. No wristband means no entrance. IQ's security team would do the scanning. Invitations were given to the entire workforce, and they were asked to request an additional wristband if needed.

IQ's two favorite reporters were asked if they wanted to come to the wedding and take photos, because he knew it would be a top story. He asked General Millworth and his wife to the wedding, as they had become friends during all the dealings IQ had with him.

He asked Albert to come to the wedding, as he had become a friend and very reliable worker. Albert said that his estranged wife had contacted him after seeing how he had straightened his life out. She said she was proud of him and thought of him often. IQ told him to invite her.

Without Ely knowing about it, he talked to his Uncle Andy and Dad about what they found out about Ely's dad. It turned out that he had been nothing but a troublemaker his whole life. He had a lengthy rap sheet and was thought to be in the area. They had photos and gave them out to security and the FBI. As they found out later, he had planned to crash the wedding and would try to insist on walking Ely down the aisle. He wanted to get back into the family's affairs and maybe get a little bit of IQ's cash, since Ely was marrying a billionaire.

IQ said, "Do whatever you have to do to keep him away from Ely and Eva."

IQ found out later that the FBI intercepted him through advanced facial recognition. They persuaded him that he would be much better off and safer on the west coast, because if they saw him anywhere near this area again, he might disappear permanently. They flew him away, and he never caused any more trouble.

Faith and Ely had a ball shopping for a wedding dress and for bridesmaids' dresses. Ely had IQ's platinum card for shopping, and he was paying for everything. Ely picked out a simple, but figure flattering white strapless gown that looked amazing with her long blonde hair, and the bridesmaids would be in different pastels. IQ picked out simple, sharp looking tan suits for the guys.

On the day of the wedding, IQ had the entire plant shut down and told everyone that they would be paid for the day off. The decorating was almost done, and the drones were ready to lift off. There were not a lot of guests for the wedding, just as Ely and IQ wanted. Grandpa and Grandma arrived by limo, and grandma was wheeled up front. She did not look well and had difficulty speaking. IQ had a corsage made especially for her and pinned it on her.

He gave her a kiss and said, "Grandma, We're so glad you could be here."

She gave a half smile and squeezed his hand a little. He had checked monthly with top researchers for a cure or even something to stave off the progression, but it was to no avail. He knew Ely would be so sad when she tried to talk with grandma. Ely had kept her promise to visit her weekly, but she came back each time more and more upset. When all the guests were ready, the music started and the Best Man and groomsmen came out and took their places next to IQ. The bridesmaids walked in slowly followed by the Maid of Honor, Faith. Ben thought she looked gorgeous and wondered about their future. Grandpa was smiling and winking at Grandma Sunny, and she gave him a half smile back. Maria turned Sunny's wheelchair towards the aisle to get a better view. Now Ely came in escorted by Danny in his full dress uniform. IQ just stared with his mouth partly open. She looked absolutely stunning with her beautiful blonde hair flowing down her back adorned with flowers woven in and her tanned bare arms and shoulders. The photographers were snapping away, and IQ was almost drooling. She had passed on wearing an old style veil, and her big blue eyes were gorgeous. They smiled at each other and held hands after Ely gave her bouquet to Faith to hold. The wedding progressed to the vows with IQ starting first.

"Ely, when I first saw you walk into our classroom, I almost instantly fell in love with you. I prayed that you didn't already have a boyfriend. When you sat alone at lunch and said it was ok to sit with you, my heart almost stopped. I found out how sweet, kind and loving you were over the days that followed and knew that I wanted you forever. Now my dream is coming true, and I promise to never hurt you or break your heart. I promise I will love you forever."

"IQ, when I first came to your school, I was so sad and depressed and had no friends. I prayed to God every night for a miracle, and he sent me a special angel with a sweet smile, a kind heart, a generous heart and a loving heart. I knew the first time that you walked me home that I wanted you forever. Now my prayers are coming true, and I promise you all the love I can give. I promise I will never hurt you or break your heart. I promise to love you forever."

Now Maria and Eva were crying silently. Grandma Sunny had tears in her eyes as did Aunt Ashley, Christy, Lea and Olive.

Grandpa called for the ring bearers, and up the aisle came Stumpy wearing a bow tie carrying a little pillow with his teeth. Alongside him came Sheba wearing a new jeweled collar carrying another pillow with her teeth. Stumpy was saying to her, "Vickie, you look awesome! Do you think they will have some food for us at the reception?"

Sheba said, "Oh my God Jim, again with the food? Yes, I'm pretty sure we can con someone into handing us some goodies, and by the way, that bow tie makes you look pretty dapper."

Faith took the ring off the pillow Sheba was carrying, and Ben took the other ring off Stumpy's pillow. Stumpy and Sheba sat down and watched the rest of the ceremony.

The exchange of rings was performed, and the pronouncing of husband and wife was followed by a long kiss. Instead of walking down the short aisle, Ely and IQ hugged and/or kissed everyone in the wedding party, thanking them and Grandpa, then they proceeded to do the same to the rest of the group in the room. IQ hugged and kissed Eva and called her Mama S. Ely went to Grandma Sunny and hugged and kissed her telling her how much she loved her. They had a half hour until the reception started, and the wedding area was quickly transformed into party central. IQ checked with the reporters and made sure they had gotten great pictures and had them take more with Danny, Maria and Eva in them. He made sure to get pictures with grandpa and grandma together with him and Ely.

IQ took Ely's hand, pulled her aside and told her how happy he was and how beautiful she looked. She told him how much she loved him and couldn't wait to get him alone. They went hand in hand towards the front door and greeted every person who arrived. The rest of the night went by in a flash with eating, dancing and singing along to the oldies. Stumpy and Sheba went around begging for food and were pretty successful.

IQ and Ely took the limo drone to the fanciest, most elegant hotel in Florida, and they had arranged for the bridal suite to be ready. Not much sleep was gotten that night.

Chapter 25
Mei Lee

IQ and Ely took a very short honeymoon. They moved to their new home with all new furnishings, and it was completely self reliant on energy. It had all the latest electronic equipment including self darkening unbreakable windows. The house was like a fortress, and it took Ely a week to figure out how to operate all of the equipment. They were trying to decide what to do with Stumpy. They knew he and Sheba were inseparable. Ely came up with a sharing plan with Christy, 4 days at one house and 3 at the other. Then they would alternate.

Christy was fine with that, but said, "Let's ask Sheba and Stumpy."

As it turned out, it was fine with the pets. They did not want to be separated. When they were brought over to the new house, they found new toys, a big new catnip doll for Sheba and a huge chew bone for Stumpy. There was also a new scratch pad for Sheba and a big sandbox. They explored the whole house and backyard. Stumpy, of course, wondered what was for dinner.

Ely and IQ had lots of work, but it was tough to resist each other on the way to Microdots in that big private drone. Ely hired one secretary, and they researched for days all of the various places and ways the substantial interest accumulating from the massive Turner Foundation could be used for the greater good. IQ, who loved children, suggested The Shriners and St. Judes. He told Ely to watch out for any organization whose top officials took home huge paychecks. He also wanted to make Florida 100% into a "No Kill" pet shelter state and would donate big bucks to those who would sign an agreement to participate. There were many individuals just looking for a few fast bucks, and Ely was good at weeding those out. He told Ely to look for schools in the state who needed supplies or free lunches for students. He told her that not all kids would have rich parents like them.

This comment caused Ely to wonder why she wasn't getting pregnant? She had stopped all birth control the day of the wedding, and their sex life was beyond wonderful. "Maybe it will be soon," she thought.

Faith called Ely often and this time told her that she and Ben had sex. She was the one who initiated it, and she used birth control. She said, "Oh Ely, it was so good, and he was so gentle and sweet. He gave me a promise ring the next day. It was all because of you, Ely. If you hadn't stopped to help me during the race, we wouldn't have become such great friends. I love you Ely and want you for my Maid of Honor if I ever get married."

Ely said she was so happy for her and she would love to be her Maid of Honor. She hoped it would be Ben.

The year flew by, and 2087 was rung in with a massive party at Microdots All the workers brought their families, and Ely noticed that the kids all flocked to "Uncle Dean," as they called him. He was so good to them all, telling them stories and doing silly magic tricks. He visited the Microdots' daycare section often to see how it was going. He would talk to Lea often, and she mentioned that she and the EMT guy, Phil, were getting serious.

Ely talked to Christy, and she told her that Joe had a scholarship at FSU and that they were getting very serious, but she wanted to concentrate on the Police Academy and SWAT training.

Harold and Olive decided to set a date to get married, much to IQ and Elys' delight.

IQ offered the huge Microdots room, but they were just going to have a very small wedding and reception. They didn't have much family and weren't into big parties or gatherings. It would be in 3 months, and they wanted IQ for a Best Man and Ely for Maid of Honor. IQ and Ely told them they were thrilled to be asked.

Ely started to worry more and more about not getting pregnant, and she pulled Olive aside one day and told her about it. Olive asked if she had ever been to a gynecologist. Ely told her no and that the only ones seemed to be men. She told her about her childhood and about getting molested by her father. She didn't want to be seen by any man other than IQ. Olive felt terrible for her and said she would do some research. She got back to Ely and said that she had located a female gynecologist who was highly respected. She said she would take Ely as a patient when Olive told her that she ran the Turner Foundation and IQ was her husband. She respected the great work that they did for children and animals.

Ely made an appointment and had tests of all kinds run. The doctor was amazed at the findings. She told Ely that she had never seen anyone in such perfect health even at her young age. She was surprised to not even find a blemish on her body of any kind. Her weight was perfect with almost no fat content. Her blood work was perfect, and the physical exam showed no abnormalities. Then she gave her the bad news. As far as they could determine, Ely was totally without eggs and unlikely to ever get pregnant. She said it was so rare that she had never seen the condition before. Usually that would indicate some other major problem, but she was in excellent condition. When she looked up, tears were streaming down Ely's face and she looked totally demoralized.

Ely said, "So I'm a freak, just like they told me in school. IQ wanted children so badly."

She put her head down and just cried away. The Doctor had kids of her own and got up and came around the table to comfort her.

"Ely, there is a way to use some other woman's eggs and fertilize them with IQ's sperm. They would then be implanted into your body."

Ely shook her head. "No, it wouldn't be ours then, just his. I have to go!"

The Doctor gave her some test kits and told her to send in a sample every month, and we just might get lucky. She felt so bad for this beautiful young girl.

Instead of heading back to the office and meeting IQ for lunch, she told the drone to go to Mama T.'s house. When she arrived at Maria and Dannys' home, no one was there but Maria who had seen the drone land from her office window. She saw Ely getting out and was happy for the visit, but then saw her crying her eyes out as she came up the front walkway.

Ely ran into her arms crying, "Mama, Mama, help me!"

Maria held her tight and sat on the big couch with her. She said, "Tell Mama what's wrong. Did IQ hurt you somehow?"

Ely was crying so hard she couldn't talk. She shook her head no. Maria hadn't seen her this upset since IQ was kidnapped. "You can tell Mama."

Ely showed her the paperwork from the doctor and gasped out, "Mama, I'm a freak, just like they used to say in school. IQ wants kids so badly. What if he doesn't want me anymore? I would just die, I would just die! He's going to hate me!"

"Oh Ely, he loves you with all his heart. He talks about how wonderful you are every time I see him. He won't hate you." She thought to herself, "God, haven't you given this young girl enough problems in her short life?"

Ely was still crying, and her whole body was shaking when suddenly another drone landed, and IQ came hurrying in.

"Ely, what's wrong? When you didn't meet me for lunch, I was so worried! I saw the drone landed here and came right over."

Maria said, "Sit here with Ely."

She got up, and IQ put his arms around Ely who was inconsolable. He just held her tight saying, "It will be ok, just tell me what's wrong. We can fix it together, just like we always do."

This just made her cry harder. She handed him the paperwork and said, "I'm so sorry IQ, I'm just a freak. Please don't hate me! I wanted to make you happy so badly."

"Ely, I love you, and I could never hate you. You are the best thing that ever happened to me. Let me read this real quick." He scanned the report, and his heart dropped. They would never have kids. "Oh Ely, I'm so sorry, but it will be ok. We have each other, and I would never get mad at you."

It took her another 10 minutes to calm down. She just lay there with her head on his chest, totally defeated. He wiped her tears away, brushed her hair back and kissed her forehead.

He said, "Ely, I have an idea. I was going to show you this before, but we were both so busy that I forgot."

He unfolded his big phone and showed her a photo. It was a picture of an adorable three year old Chinese-American girl. She had big brown eyes and was smiling. IQ told Ely that the school she was in was a type of orphanage for unwanted children. He told her that there was still a stigma in some areas that girl children were somehow less desirable than boys and in particular, one fathered by an American. He said that she had a birth defect, her left foot was missing just like Stumpy. The owner of the school said she was very intelligent and called her precocious. Her name was Mei Lee, meaning beautiful in Chinese. She was available for adoption.

"Ely, If you want to meet her, we can fly to the west coast in a couple of hours by supersonic jet. Think about it for a few days."

Ely looked at the picture and smiled just a tiny bit. "I don't know IQ, can we go home now?"

"Sure Ely, it's been a rough day. I'll take off the rest of the day also."

They headed home, and Ely went into the bedroom and laid down. IQ could hear her sobbing quietly and didn't know what to do. He called Harold and told him he was taking off for a few days and that Ely had gotten some bad news. He would explain later. He went out into the lanai and called his Mom. He said, "Mom, for once in my life I don't know what to do to make it better. Her heart is broken."

She said, "IQ, just give her a couple of days to process everything. She may get back to her happy, sweet self."

When IQ went to bed, Ely was facing away from him and crying very softly. IQ rolled over, gave her a kiss on the cheek and told her he loved her and that they could talk in the morning. All he heard was a very soft ok. In the morning when IQ woke up, Ely was out of bed and sitting out in the lanai just staring at the retention pond with all the wading birds. She had a sad look on her face. IQ gave her a kiss on the cheek, but she didn't say anything or respond in any way, just stared.

He said, "Ely honey, can I get you some coffee or hot tea?"

Ely said quietly, "No thanks. IQ, why did God make me this way? I pray every day, I try to be kind to everyone. I try to be helpful and loving. It's not fair."

She sounded like she might cry again, and IQ sat down and put his arms around her.

IQ said, "I asked myself that same thing when I was in grade school. I had that wild red hair, big thick glasses, and was short and skinny. I looked at Ben and Christy and they were both big, good looking and tough. I just don't know, but don't ever think that I don't love you just the way you are. I meant every single word of my vows when we got married."

This time he got a kiss from Ely. They took another couple of days off, but IQ was afraid to start anything sexual, because he didn't know what kind of reaction he would get. He would wait until she made some kind of move. Ely looked at the picture of Mei Lee several times and wondered how it would feel to hold her in her arms and maybe get hugs and kisses. She was worried about IQ, because he hadn't seemed to want to have sex with her for days. She decided to see if he still wanted her and got in bed completely naked. When IQ got in bed a little later, he rolled over to give her a kiss.

She turned to him and said, "Hold me close."

IQ got quite a surprise and said, "Ely, are you sure you are ready? I didn't want to upset you, but I wanted you so badly!"

She just said, "Take off those PJs."

The sex was slower and more tender each time that night, and they slept in each other's arms.

In the morning, Ely said, "I think I would like to meet Mei Lee. Could we go today?"

IQ said, "I'll charter a plane if I can't get seats on the supersonic jet."

He was excited that Ely seemed to be getting better. There were two seats left in the very expensive first class section, but IQ just shrugged and booked them. His platinum card was the only one with no limit. He gave a quick call to Harold and told him what they were doing. Harold told him everything was running smoothly and another order for 100 "Grey Ghost" devices may be coming. That would be a 50 billion dollar order. IQ was shocked that the government would put out that amount. The device must be proving quite useful.

He said, "Great job Harold and Olive. Thank you for running the company so well while I'm gone."

Harold said, "We've got your back anytime. Just take care of Ely."

The plane landed in Los Angeles, and IQ had a limo service all ready to take them to the orphanage. Upon arrival they were greeted by the manager, and he explained how they operated. He also said they were at capacity and were running short of cash. IQ told him that they could help with that, but he wanted to look around at how it was being run and meet Mei Lee. The manager told them that Mei Lee had been disappointed so many times, but she didn't give up on getting parents. She was so cute and smart, but prospective clients looked at her missing foot and weren't interested.

Mei Lee was at a table coloring in a book when Ely and IQ entered. She glanced up and smiled. Her hair was in pigtails with pink ribbons, and she looked adorable. Ely's heart went out to her when she looked under the table and saw her left leg in just a type of sock. IQ and Ely were introduced, and Mei Lee looked from one to the other saying to Ely, "You have pretty eyes."

Ely replied, "So do you, Mei Lee, and I like your pigtails."

Mei Lee beamed and held out her arms to get picked up. Ely picked her up, and Mei Lee hugged her tightly. She said, "You smell so nice, just like flowers."

IQ was thinking that this little girl could really talk well for her age, almost adult like. He glanced at what she was coloring, and it was done perfectly, staying in all the lines. Mei Lee even printed her name neatly on the page. He was thinking, no way at this age and asked the manager about it. He said, "Yes, she knows the alphabet, many big words, songs and can count to one hundred. She picks up things so quickly."

IQ said, "Mei Lee, can I hold you next?"

She held out her arms to IQ, and he held her close. He told her that he liked her coloring a lot, and she was very smart to be able to write her name like that. She said, "Thank you, I love Cinderella coloring books."

Ely had a big smile on her face and a tear in her eye. She said, "Would you like us to be your mommy and daddy?"

IQ was shocked, Mei Lee had made quite the impression on her. Mei Lee looked from one to the other with a strange expression on her face. She looked at the manager, and he explained that she had been disappointed so many times when people saw her leg. Ely held out her left hand and showed Mei Lee. Her eyes got even bigger, and she said, "Ely was hurt?" She reached out to touch Ely's hand.

Ely said, "No Mei Lee, I was born that way."

Mei Lee said, "I was born this way." She held up her leg.

IQ gave her back to Ely and said, "Mei Lee, I want to show you some pictures." He opened his large phone and showed her pictures of Stumpy with his left paw missing and then with the new one in place. He said, "This is our dog Stumpy, and he was born without a left foot too, but we made him one that looks almost perfect. We can make one to fit you too. We will make you new ones as you get bigger, if you want us for your mommy and daddy."

Mei Lee had tears of joy in her eyes, and said, "Yes, I really, really want you as my mommy and daddy. I'll be very good. You won't have to holler at me. I promise."

Ely said, "We will take really good care of you, and we won't ever holler at you."

Mei Lee hugged and kissed Ely and IQ.

IQ said, "How long would the adoption take to process?"

The manager said that her adoption was a special case because she had waited so long and that they could do it that day. He had already checked out Ely and IQs' immaculate background, and they certainly had the means to take care of her. IQ said he would donate $5 million immediately to the orphanage, and they could look for his support in the future. He showed the manager pictures of their home which looked like a mini mansion and told him that Mei Lee would have her own bedroom, full bathroom and playroom and would want for nothing ever again. He asked how Mei Lee was getting around the facility, and the manager showed him a mini walker and a crutch that she sometimes used. IQ asked if he could sign the paperwork right away and get all her personal belongings, medical records and birth certificate. He told Ely to take Mei Lee to her room and get all her belongings ready to go, then meet him in the office for her signature or signatures on the paperwork. While they were getting the paperwork together, IQ called Harold and told him to wire $5 million to the account of the orphanage immediately. IQ chartered a plane just for the three of them to take off in 3 hours. Ely took Mei Lee to her very sparse room and asked what clothes and other things she had. There were hardly any items, and Ely told her that they were going shopping tomorrow for pretty new clothes, coloring books and toys.

Mei Lee said, "I love you, Mommy. Oh, and Daddy too."

After all the paperwork was signed and IQ made sure the cash was in the orphanage's account, they shook hands with the manager and told him they were grateful for the speedy work. He thanked them for the generous donation and said they would use the money for much needed improvements. A limo was called, and the three of them headed for the airport. IQ asked Mei Lee if she had ever flown in an airplane, and she said no. He told her it was fun, and she would be above the clouds and able to look down on them. He said the cars, houses and people look like little tiny toys from way up there. He said when she got tired of looking out the window, she could play games on his big phone or even take a nap if she wanted to. He showed her a picture of their big house and said she would have her own big bedroom, bathroom and a playroom. Mei Lee stared at him and smiled. On the plane, Ely texted Olive, told her the news and asked if she would make a quick store trip and rush the items to their house. She gave Olive the house code.

Harold and Olive were amazed at the speed of the adoption process, and Harold said, "Money talks and bullshit walks I guess."

Mei Lee was fascinated looking out the window of the plane and spent most of the time looking down and pointing out everything. She finally took a nap on Ely's lap, with her head resting against Ely's chest. Ely stroked her hair with a contented look on her face and a smile every so often at IQ. They took Microdots' large drone from the airport to their house and landed in the wide driveway. Mei Lee stared at the huge house and asked if it was all theirs. Ely told her yes, and she would have her very own rooms and a big girl bed. She hoped

Olive was successful in finding what she asked for. IQ put Mei Lee on his shoulders and gave her a tour of the whole house. He asked if she knew how to swim and showed her the big pool and spa. She was looking at everything with her big brown eyes wide open and told him no.

He said, "We will teach you, but don't go near the pool alone until you learn how."

She said, "Ok, Daddy."

He handed her off to Ely, who said, "Would you like to see your rooms?"

"Oh yes, Mommy."

When they showed her the bedroom, they found that Olive had successfully found all Cinderella bedding and made the beds. Mei Lee squealed with joy and was laughing, hugging and kissing Ely. Olive had also found a small Cinderella desk and chair. It had several coloring and workbooks already on it with colored pencils and crayons. Mei Lee was clapping her hands and laughing in delight. She asked her new daddy and mommy to come closer for a kiss, and they all had a group kiss. They found out that Mei Lee liked just about every type of food, so they had supper delivered. IQ told Mei Lee that as soon as they could arrange it, she would be getting a new foot and walking around on her own.

IQ was keeping an eye on Ely, because he knew how upset she had been, but she seemed pretty good. He would talk to her at bedtime. The doorbell rang, and it was Christy with Stumpy and Sheba. Ely and IQ had forgotten it was their turn to take care of them. Christy was shocked to see Mei Lee, but recovered quickly when she heard the story. She held out her arms and said, "I'm your Auntie Christy. Can I give you a hug?"

Mei Lee hugged her and kissed her on the cheek. Mei Lee said, "Auntie Christy, is that 'Umpy'?"

Stumpy said, "Look Vickie, how cute she is, and she called me, 'Umpy.'"

Sheba was behind him and Mei Lee said, "Oh, a big kitty, so pretty."

Christy was smiling and said, "Yes, That's Stumpy, and the kitty is called Sheba. It's their turn to stay here for a few days."

Vickie said, "Jim, you know I don't much like little kids, but this one has love coming off her in waves. Ely said they got her at an orphanage. Did you overhear Maria telling Danny that Ely couldn't have children?"

"Oh no," said Jim. "So that's why Maria has been so upset lately. Should we ask Bill up in Level 2 if he could help in some way?"

"We could try, but that's a big ask!"

"Look Vickie, Mei Lee has a left foot missing, just like me. I bet IQ will fix it. Let's be really nice to her, the poor thing."

"Ok Jim, I'll be on my best behavior, as Lea always tells us to be at the daycare."

Mei Lee asked to get down on the floor to pet the two giant animals. She could kneel on that leg and was petting both of them at the same time. "Mommy and Daddy, I love them so much. Can they sleep in my room tonight so I feel safe?"

Ely said, "They can actually understand English. Try asking them."

Mei Lee did, and they both nodded yes. She asked Stumpy if she could look at his paw, and he held it up. She looked it over and felt it and told him that Daddy was going to make her a foot, but not with fur. Ely, IQ and Christy laughed.

Christy had to go, but she told them she would take the pets for a while if they were too much to handle. Christy hustled back to her house and found her mom and dad out on the lanai. She said, "Did you know that Ely and IQ adopted a child? Why didn't you tell me before I dropped off the pets?"

Maria jumped up and said, "They did what? They didn't even tell us that they were considering it. Do they have the child already?"

Christy said, "Yes Mom, it's an adorable little three + year old girl, called Mei Lee. She is as sharp as a whip and talks better than some of the guys I dated. They flew to California today and got her from an orphanage. She has a birth defect. She was born without a left foot, just like Stumpy. IQ plans to fix it asap."

Danny, who rarely curses, said, "Christy, are you shitting us?"

"No Dad, I'm 'serious as a heart attack,' like grandpa always says."

Maria was already on the phone and calling IQ.

IQ said to Ely, "Uh Oh, It's Mom. Christy squealed on us." He said, "Mei Lee, would you like to say hi to your new grandma?" He set the big screen to video mode. Then he hit the answer button.

Maria was suddenly looking at a sweet little girl who was blowing her kisses and saying, "Hi Grandma, I'm Mei Lee." That's all it took for Maria to fall in love with her.

Maria said, "Hi Mei Lee, I can't wait to see you and give you a hug."

Danny decided he might as well get in on the action and turned Maria's phone slightly to say, "Hi Mei Lee, I'm your new grandpa, and I would love to give you a hug in person. Come see us soon."

"Hi Grandpa." Mei Lee blew more kisses.

Ely took the phone and told them that they had a very busy day scheduled tomorrow, as Mei Lee needed all new clothes and a bunch of other things. She would also need to get measured for a new foot, but they would come visit as soon as they could. She asked if they would tell Ashley and Andy about their new grand niece and tell Ben he was an uncle and Lea an aunt. They would come to see them soon.

Ely and IQ were both exhausted, and Mei Lee looked tired, so Ely said she would give her a bath and put her in the only PJs she owned.

Mei Lee said to Ely, "Mommy, I can use the potty all by myself."

Ely said, "That's wonderful, I'm so proud of you."

While Ely was getting her ready for bed, IQ dragged the two pet beds into Mei Lee's room and put one on each side. He took Stumpy and Sheba out for their nightly ritual and told them to protect Mei Lee. They both nodded yes. Mei Lee was thrilled when she saw one pet on each side of the bed. Ely and IQ kissed her goodnight and told her they would be right in the next room. They told her to call out to them if she needed to use the potty and that Sheba and Stumpy would protect her. She quickly fell fast asleep. Ely and IQ got in bed, discussed everything and made plans for the next day.

Ely told him how much she loved him, and they quietly made out for quite a while. The next day was a whirlwind of activity, and Ely had Olive accompany her and Mei Lee to shop. IQ told his specialty shop he wanted a foot made by the end of the day. They had taken molds and measurements of Mei Lee's leg and suggested an easily removable foot and ankle with external feedback sensors, so that they could remove it for baths or to use the pool.

IQ said, "You guys rock, and there will be big bonus checks for you if this is ready today." The foot was ready and fit perfectly. The team said that adjustments could be made every month to compensate for growth. IQ wrote generous bonus checks out on the spot.

Mei Lee was delighted, and said, "Daddy, I can feel my new foot touching things. I love you so much!"

IQ was thrilled and told her it might take a while to get used to the new foot, but she was walking almost normally in just a few minutes.

The Microdots' employees all fell in love with her. She loved Auntie Lea and commented on her beautiful red hair. She loved going to the daycare, and she would make stories up to tell the other kids and would read children's books to them.

Maria went bonkers over her and told Ely and IQ that they did a wonderful thing saving her from the orphanage. The only sad day came when Ely took her to see Grandma Sunny. Ely warned her that her great grandma was very old, very sick and had trouble talking, moving her arms and hands and could no longer walk.

Mei Lee said with a very serious look on her face, "I will talk to her and hug and kiss her then."

Great Grandpa loved her from the start. Mei Lee walked over to where Sunny was sitting and crawled up on the couch next to her. She hugged her with her little arms and gave her a kiss on the cheek. She called her Great Grandma. She showed her the new foot Daddy had made for her and explained all about it. She told her she was learning to swim and all about playing with Stumpy and Sheba. She chattered away for a long time with Sunny nodding and smiling.

She held Sunny's hand and innocently said, "Maybe my Daddy could fix you too?"

Ely's eyes started tearing up and Mei Lee looked at her and said, "Did Mei Lee say something wrong?"

Sunny was able to get out a soft "No, honey" with a smile.

Ely told Mei Lee that her great grandma needed to rest and that they would come back another day. Mei Lee hugged and kissed her cheek again and said, "I love you, Great Grandma. I will read you a story book next time we come." She went out to hug her great grandpa.

Ely was wiping tears away when she kissed grandma, and Sunny just nodded and was able to whisper, "It's ok dear. She is so precious."

Ely was crying in the drone and Mei Lee asked why. "Is Mommy mad at Mei lee?"

"Oh honey, never. I'm just sad that your great grandma is so sick. I'll show you pictures from when she and your great grandpa were young when we get home."

The rest of the year flew by. Microdots was doing amazingly well and was so profitable that employees would be getting large end of the year bonuses from IQ. Another massive contract had been signed with the government.

Ely was running the Turner foundation very efficiently, and the net worth was actually growing, even though large donations were being made to many organizations and people who had suffered great loss. When she got to the office after lunch one day, she saw that framed pictures of her were on the wall surrounding her Good Sportsmanship award. There were several pictures of her playing tennis and some of her hopping the net to congratulate the other players. Others showed her helping Faith across the finish line and one of her holding an ice pack on Faith's leg. Others showed her winning races by a huge margin and some showed her cheering other runners on. She found out that IQ had been in that day when she was out to lunch with Olive and put them up. Her secretary told her that he said he was so proud of her and loved her so much. Ely walked across the building to his office and sat on his lap, kissing him and telling him how much she loved him. She said she should have worn her "Hooker Outfit," but she would reward him later that night in bed.

Mei Lee turned 4 and a big party was held at Danny and Marias' home. Ely and IQ were teaching her all kinds of things, and it appeared that she might be in the genius category herself. She was learning stuff that 3rd and 4th graders were being taught. They discussed homeschooling her, but were undecided. IQ said they could split the daycare into part schooling and part daycare for the younger kids and could hire bonafide teachers. Ely proclaimed it a great idea, and it was implemented. This way they could work together and keep an eye on her.

Olive and Harold had gotten married and were loving life. They had purchased a new home and had been discussing having children. Olive told him that she was worried that Ely would be hurt if she got pregnant too quickly, so they decided to wait a while.

Ely's Mom, Eva, was still seeing Manny, and she was falling in love with him. Ely knew he was a good man and had high hopes for them.

Ben and Christy had completed the Police Academy with top honors and were both in Danny's command. They were doing a great job. Christy was in the SWAT division, and Ben had already been promoted to detective. Ben planned to propose to Faith on Christmas Eve, but decided to keep it a secret from Ely since they were close friends. Joe was kicking butt in college football and studying Criminology, which he enjoyed very much. He took IQ's graduation speech to heart and was getting top grades. He and Christy were still together.

Lea and her EMT guy, Phil, were still seeing each other and were discussing marriage and which way her career was going. He was head over heels in love with her.

Maria, Danny, Ashley and Andy were going out to supper one evening, and they discussed how well the whole family was doing and how they loved Mei Lee. She was very intelligent, and Ely had snapped a picture of her reading to her great grandma Sunny, just like she said she would do. They all were extremely concerned about Sunny, as she was losing weight and was not able to swallow well. They said how Ely would show up crying after a visit with Sunny, with Mei Lee trying to comfort her, instead of the other way around.

Christmas and New Year's Eve came and went. IQ and Ely gave out very expensive presents, with Mom and Dad and Uncle Andy and Aunt Ashley getting a small box to open for each couple. When they opened them, they found just a key fob. They were at their mom and dad's, so they told them to push the button and go outside. Within five minutes a large new fancy drone approached and landed in the driveway. It had their names on the outside and the lighted Microdots symbol on both sides and underneath. It was the most plush model ever made. They looked at IQ and Ely who were smiling. They said, it's yours Mom and Dad and told Uncle Andy and Aunt Ashley they had an identical one and to try it out later. When you need a ride, just push the button and the drone will find you. Get in and tell it where you want to go. At night, hit the button again, and it will go back and recharge itself at Microdots. You will never be charged again for any service. Both couples were speechless and thanked Ely and IQ over and over. Lea, Ben and Christy were given cards that gave free taxi drone rides whenever they needed them. Just call and one will show up and you swipe the card. There would never be a charge for them. They were engraved with "Team Badass" and their names. Another group hug for "Team Badass" was given. Eva was also given a fancy engraved card with her name for free taxi drone rides for two to anywhere she wanted to go in the USA.

Faith called Ely on Christmas Day and was so excited. Ben had proposed to her and had given her a beautiful engagement ring. Ely was so happy for her and Ben.

IQ said, "I can't believe it. The big stud bites the dust."

Ely laughed and gave him a whack on the shoulder.

Chapter 26
The Year 2088

It was March 1st and a gorgeous day in Florida. Ely was sitting out in the lanai with Stumpy and Sheba, but they could feel the sadness in her. IQ had taken Mei Lee to school at Microdots after Ely told him she would come later, because she wanted to feed the pets first. She adored Mei Lee, but really wanted to give IQ their own baby. She was sending in the test kits monthly that the gynecologist had given her, but to no avail.

Stumpy said, "Vickie, I bet she is thinking again about why she can't have a child."

"Yes Jim, I believe you're right. Let's contact Bill in Level 2 again and see if he can finally help."

Stumpy said, "Bill, Bill, are you there?"

Bill replied, "Yes Jim, and Hi Vickie. I know what you are going to ask, but miracles take time. There are millions a day being requested. I even asked my trainer, Johnnie, in Level 1 for help. He told me that things are looking up, so maybe."

Stumpy said, "Thanks Bill, nobody is more deserving than Ely in our opinion." He went over to Ely, put his huge head on her lap and looked up.

Ely said, "I bet you know what I'm thinking, but I'll be ok. Let's get ready to go to the daycare and make some kids happy. Sheba, IQ told me he put up a very tall climbing post for you with a big nest on top, so you can hide from the kids when they annoy you."

IQ, Harold and Olive were churning out ideas and new products by the dozens and also worked on improving their older designs. The world seemed like a calmer place now that the "Grey Ghosts" were being used. They were able to lower the prices for the government with improved manufacturing. More orders rolled in like clockwork, so they knew the devices were being used to good effect. Microdots products were world renowned for their quality and excellent guarantees. They sold 50 "Buzz Juniors" to the government, and they were used to varying degrees of success. They were so tiny, that a couple got sucked into ventilation ducts and probably ended up in the AC filters. Some were used in outside breezes even after the strict warnings by IQ and ended up far from their intended destinations. Some did exactly what General Millworth wanted them to, and he was highly pleased. Harold had almost perfected another device to be used along with "Buzz." It was almost ready, but he wanted to surprise IQ.

Andy, Ashley, Danny and Maria had gone to the old Sawgrass Grove area where nightly bands played for the last 65 plus years. Danny and Ashleys' dad had called them and said that Sunny wanted to go one last time, because that's where they had their first date. He asked if they would go along. They were shocked by their mom's condition. She was very thin, very weak and could no longer speak. She seemed to go downhill by the week, and Ashley, in particular, was very near to tears.

Another two months went by, and Danny and Ashley got the call from their dad that they had been dreading. He could barely get out the words that their mom, Sunny, had died. They rushed over and found their dad, BD, absolutely inconsolable. Cremation had been pre-arranged, and that went forward. They were able to set up a plan to text or call their dad daily. He told them about the last few minutes of his beloved Sunny's life and what had happened. The 4 grandkids were notified. They had all expected it to happen soon, but were still very upset. When IQ told Ely, she was devastated and wondered how she could tell Mei Lee that the only great grandma that she had ever known had died. Ely went over to the daycare and school section and got Mei Lee out of class. They went to a vacant office, and Mei Lee saw that Ely had tears in her eyes.

She said, "Mommy, don't cry. Is it because of my great grandma again?"

Ely's voice cracked when she replied, "Yes honey, she died this morning, and we won't be able to visit her again, only to see your great grandpa."

Mei Lee asked, "Did my great grandma go to heaven?"

"Yes sweetheart, I'm sure she did. She won't have anymore pain and will look young again, like in the pictures I showed you."

"Mommy, well then I will talk to her up there when we pray together." She handed Ely some tissues from a box on the desk and put out her arms for a hug.

Ely picked her up and hugged her tightly saying, "I love you Mei Lee and so did your great grandma."

"I know she did. Mommy, you're squeezing the stuffing out of me. It's my turn to read to the class soon. Can we go back now? I'll be ok."

Ely had to smile and said, "Sure, and thank you for making me feel better."

"Mommy, I'll read just like I'm talking to my great grandma."

Ely gave her kisses all the way back to the classroom. When IQ asked how it went, Ely said, "She actually made 'me' feel better. She's going to be a real Pip, as grandma used to say."

Three days later, the family got another shock when Danny and Ashley found their dad after he didn't respond to their texts and calls. This time IQ decided to tell Mei Lee.

He went to the classroom and told the teacher what had happened. He picked up Mei Lee and gave her a kiss. He said, "Something very sad happened. Your great grandpa was so very, very sad, that he decided to go to heaven and be with your great grandma. We won't be able to go see them anymore at their house. I'm sorry Mei Lee, they loved you very much."

Mei Lee's face got a very serious look on it, and she thought for a short while. "Great Grandpa and Great Grandma are together now, and they both look young like in the pictures Mommy showed me?"

"Yes Mei Lee, we are sure they are."

"Daddy, can I be sad and happy at the same time?"

"Yes, I feel that way myself sweetie."

"I love you Daddy, and I will read stories to both of them now." She hugged him and went back to class.

A couple of weeks later, Danny and Ashley picked up the urns with the ashes. They had asked The Villages for a special area for a memorial bench and plaques in a beautiful location along the Hawkins Walking Trail. IQ paid 10 times the amount so they would do a rush job. Condolences came in from everywhere, and the news media ran several major stories about all the good things that Sunny and BD had accomplished over the 65 years they were together. The family requested that any donations be put toward finding a cure for ALS once and for all. Microdots' Turner Foundation had been donating millions toward that for years.

A date was picked for the family to meet up at the memorial bench for the spreading of the ashes. It would only be for the immediate family. IQ wanted Ely to come, because she was so close to his grandparents. Mei Lee asked what was going to happen, so IQ and Ely explained about cremation and how her great grandparents were no longer using their old bodies. Instead, they had new younger bodies and were together in heaven.

They were very happy there. Mei Lee gave this great thought for quite a while. Then she said, "I think I understand, and I want to come and say goodbye, but I'm still going to keep reading to them."

"Mei Lee, that will be wonderful and so nice of you," Ely said.

Plans were made to meet up in the morning. Ely would bring Mei Lee and Stumpy. IQ had to make a quick stop at his office and would meet them there.

Ben had some exciting news he wanted to spring on everybody when they got together. He and Faith would be getting married at the end of June. He had previously told Ely that he never met anyone as sweet and loving as Faith, and he thanked her for introducing them. She would be so excited to hear about the wedding.

Christy had good news of her own. She planned to show off her new engagement ring from Joe. They were going to wait to get married until he graduated from college while she kept up with her advanced SWAT training. She had just made Lieutenant and wanted to advance even higher. She asked Sheba if she wanted to come but told her it was a long walk. Sheba knew Stumpy was coming, so she nodded yes.

Lea was going to spring her own good news. Phil had asked her to marry him and had given her an expensive engagement ring.

It was early in the morning when Ely got a call from her gynecologist. She was told that she would be getting a package in 15 minutes by drone and to look the contents over very carefully. She was told to come in as soon as possible for an appointment. The gynecologist had to take another call and told Ely to just read the report and look in the package. She was smiling when she hung up the phone.

Ely was filled with dread. What if there was something wrong and she was sick. She waited anxiously for the drone. Mei Lee was up and asked what was going on and why Mommy looked so worried. Ely told her a doctor was sending something, and she was a little worried that she might have something wrong with her. Mei Lee told her that she and Daddy would take care of her.

Ely thought, "God, I love this child so much," and picked her up for some hugs and kisses.

The drone was right on time, and Ely quickly grabbed the small package. Inside were some reports and a small box like the one she would dutifully send in every month. Stumpy had awakened and came plodding out, hungry as usual. He wondered what the commotion was about. He missed Sheba, who Christy had kept overnight after a late veterinarian visit. Ely read the first page of the reports and couldn't believe her eyes. She quickly opened the box and looked at the test kit. It was the one she had just sent in, and it read positive. Ely was pregnant, but there were both a pink plus and a blue plus. She excitedly read the next page. It said she was one month pregnant with twins, a boy and a girl and that the results had been triple checked for accuracy. With the most modern technology being used, they appeared to be in perfect condition. Ely started crying and laughing at the same time. She picked up Mei Lee and spun her around a couple of times.

Stumpy and Mei Lee were baffled, and Mei Lee asked, "So, is Mommy ok?"

"Yes, Mommy is very ok, better than ok! Mommy is going to have twin babies."

Mei Lee looked very unusual, almost like she wanted to cry, which happened very rarely. She asked, "Are Mommy and Daddy going to send Mei Lee away and back to the orphanage?"

Ely quickly picked her up again and said, "Oh, never, never, never! Daddy and I searched for the perfect little girl all over the world, and then we finally found you. We love you and want you to be a big sister to your baby brother and baby sister. You can teach them all kinds of things and even how to read when they get old enough." The relief was evident in Mei Lee's expression. She said, "Mei Lee will be a great big sister and help Mommy with everything."

Stumpy did his version of the happy dance and said, "Vickie, can you hear me? Great news, Ely is pregnant with twins."

Vickie replied, "Wow, fantastic, Johnnie must have come through for us in Level 1. We have to thank him. Bill, can you reach Johnnie in Level 1 and thank him that Ely is pregnant."

Bill said, "That's fantastic news, but Ely must have done it on her own, because Johnnie couldn't help."

Ely said, "Mei Lee, we are really going to surprise Daddy this morning. We will give him the report and the box and watch his reaction."

She and Mei Lee got dressed in identical spring dresses. She gave Stumpy his favorite breakfast and told him to hustle outside and do his business. They would be late if they didn't hurry. She would let the clean up robot take care of the back yard. She called for a high speed 4 passenger drone.

IQ arrived at the Memorial bench area and had two packages of his own. He planned to surprise Ely and Mei Lee with gifts, because he knew they were both still a little sad over the loss of his grandparents. He removed a drone from his small backpack and got it ready. He greeted everybody warmly. Nobody had sprung their surprises yet. Everyone was waiting for Ely, Stumpy and Mei Lee to arrive. IQ got a message from Ely that the drone had to land near the start of the trail and that they were walking toward them. IQ was a nervous wreck and always worried about Ely and Mei Lees' safety. Now they had to walk quite a ways with Stumpy and Mei Lee both having artificial left feet. He felt better when he saw a large FBI drone hovering and watching over them. He got his gifts ready and sent them towards the threesome. They came into sight, and he saw Mei Lee riding on Stumpy's back like he was a pony. He had to laugh, but he worried a little about Stumpy's paw.

Ely saw the drone approaching and noticed it was carrying something. It landed in front of her, and she untied the two boxes. She made it look like she was having trouble undoing the strings, but she was really tying on her own surprise for the return trip. She couldn't wait to see his expression. She had never been this happy since the wedding night.

She and Mei Lee opened the gifts. They were identical bracelets made of solid gold, heart shaped links and matched Ely's necklace. They both fit perfectly. They both waved, and Ely made a heart shape with her hands.

Mei Lee said, "Daddy really loves us."

Ely relied, "He sure does. The drone is almost back to him. Let's keep walking and watch. This should be fun."

IQ saw something hanging on the drone and wondered what it could possibly be. He quickly untied the package and opened it up. He opened the box first and saw a big plus sign next to a blue plus and a pink plus. He thought, "Could it be, could it really be?" He read the report and started running around like a wild man showing it to everybody. He thought. "Oh my God, I'm going to be the Father of twins!"

The whole group was cheering, waving, hugging and dancing around. Suddenly IQ was actually crying a little, which hadn't happened since he was 2 or 3 years old. He said, "Mom, I'm so happy."

Maria hugged him and started calculating what month she could start holding the babies.

Mei Lee was laughing and clapping her hands. Ely was grinning from ear to ear, and said, "We sure surprised them."

Stumpy actually barked, which he rarely did. He couldn't do the happy dance, because he might throw Mei Lee off his back. He was a little peeved that he didn't get a gift though. Ely saw IQ running down the trail towards them. He quickly got there and hugged and kissed Ely. She saw he had tears in his eyes. He turned around and plucked Mei Lee off of Stumpy, saying, "You're going to be a big sister."

He put her up on his shoulders to ride the rest of the way. He put his arm around Ely and said, "I can't begin to tell you how happy I am and how proud of you I am."

She said, "It took the two of us. The doctor said it was a one in a million chance. I'm going to pray my heart out. I think grandma and grandpa helped."

When they got to the group, there was a lot of hugging and kissing all around. The other three members of "Team Badass" said, "We also have some surprises for you."

The two girls held out their hands with their new engagement rings showing. Ben told them he couldn't show them anything, but that he and Faith were getting married at the end of June. There was another round of celebrating. What was originally going to be a sad gathering had turned into a joyous celebration. Danny and Andy were wishing they had brought cigars to light up, just like when they solved a big case.

Stumpy said, "Sheba, did you get any treats?"

"Oh boy, here we go again. Didn't you have a big breakfast?"

"Yes, but I need something to tide me over."

Suddenly, IQ remembered something and picked up his backpack. He pulled out a package of meat type treats and said to the pets, "I almost forgot your treats with all the excitement." He gave each of them a treat.

Stumpy said to Sheba, "See Vickie, good old IQ didn't forget us."

Vickie said, "You were right Jim. I love this family. Can you feel the big change in Ely and IQ. They are so incredibly happy."

"Yes Vickie, and the rest of the group is feeling really good, especially Maria. Did I tell you about the fun thing we are going to do later? I talked to Bill about it, so watch what happens."

The sky had been clouding over while everyone was celebrating all the good news. Danny said, "We better sprinkle the ashes before it showers. We can go back to our house to celebrate all the good news after that."

Danny and Ashley had everyone gather around the memorial bench and hold hands. Danny asked Maria to say a prayer, because she was always so good at it during gatherings.

Maria said, "God, we thank you for the very long lives, love and happiness of Sunny and BD. Please remember the many times they have touched other peoples' lives and for their unconditional love for their family. As we scatter these ashes, we release our dear ones into your loving hands where they truly belong. Thank you for filling us with the hope of seeing them again when we come home to be with you. Let your love fill the void in our hearts, and help us always remember the joy we found in the times we shared with them.

"We also ask for blessings for their beloved pets whose ashes we will scatter with them. Please remember them for the three lives that they saved and the many children they helped. In Jesus' name we pray. Amen."

Suddenly, a single ray of sunshine broke through the clouds and lit up the memorial bench as everyone was saying how beautiful Maria's words were. When Danny and Ashley were scattering the ashes behind the bench under an oak tree, 4 more rays of light broke through the clouds and lit up the urns. This got everyone's attention, especially IQ's.

Vickie said, "Jim, did you and Bill plan that? It was beautiful."

"Yes Vickie, and something else a little more fun is coming."

While the gathering was getting ready to break up, a couple with two dogs came towards them on the path. Sheba said, "Oh No Stumpy, do those mind tricks still work?"

Stumpy said, "Yes, it's been set up with Bill. This is the fun part."

Ashley and Danny were talking after the scattering of the ashes and looked up at the approaching dogs. Ashley said, "Danny, they look just like Chewie and Braveheart. The German Shepherd has the same gold paws and a gold spot on his chest, and the Golden looks exactly like Chewie looks in the old pictures. It's uncanny!"

"Sis, you're right, let's say Hi."

The couple stopped to talk, and Stumpy and Sheba greeted the two dogs like old friends. The couple commented on the sizes of Sheba and Stumpy and how friendly they were. They told Danny they were from out of town and just renting for a month. Danny gave them one of his cards and told them to call if they encountered any problems. They thanked him and expressed sincere condolences when told about the gathering. They told them that they had rescued their two dogs and that they were pretty smart. After chatting a little more they continued their walk around the wetlands.

Back at Microdots, Harold and Olive were searching frantically for a missing "Buzz" drone that Harold had on his desk in the morning. It had the special invention attached to it that he was ready to show IQ. Harold said that IQ must have picked it up thinking it was just another model ready to use. No one else could access their private offices except IQ and Ely. The very small combination landing pad, card reader and storage box was missing. IQ must have silenced his phone, as Harold couldn't get in touch with him. He left a message telling him to call as soon as possible. Harold was sweating bullets because it had cost hundreds of thousands of dollars to produce just one tiny attachment for "Buzz."

Danny and Ashley were among the last to leave. IQ and Ely were still hugging and kissing on the new memorial bench and making plans for the new additions that would be coming in 8 months. Maria had taken Mei Lee. Danny glanced across the wetlands and did a double take. Although a long distance away, he could swear that the two dogs they had just met were sitting down and saluting him. Their owners had stopped to talk to another couple. Ashley couldn't quite make it out, so Danny ran over to IQ and asked him to send the drone up for a look.

IQ said, "Dad, that is just a very cheap delivery drone without a camera system or recording capability. Are you sure you weren't just wishful thinking?"

Stumpy and Sheba were laughing hysterically. "Oh my God

Stumpy, that was a good one. You're a real brat."

"Sheba my dear, we have to keep him on his toes."

IQ suddenly said, "Wait, we might be able to use a 'Buzz' model I picked up off Harold's desk this morning. There's not too much breeze, so it might have enough charge to make it over and back." He got the small box out of his knapsack and carefully activated the tiny drone. It looked just a little bit different than normal, and it only had a 25 % charge, so maybe it would make it over and back and record some footage. He sent it up and headed it toward the group on the far bank. When it got halfway across against a stiffer breeze that had come up, it read about 15 %. He said, "Dad, we have to start it back or we'll lose it." He had been recording and he headed back, but doubted the front facing camera would have gotten much of anything.

Suddenly Danny said, "There, there, they're doing it again!"

IQ was too busy worrying about retrieving the drone, and Ely was excitedly talking to her Mom on her phone about her becoming a grandmother to twins. Ashley still couldn't quite make it out, but the dogs were certainly doing something. IQ was just able to retrieve the drone near the water's edge. He synced it to his phone and got a video of only a few seconds of the dogs just sitting there facing them and staring. He showed his Dad and said, "I'm sorry Dad. If we had expected something out of the ordinary, I would have brought a better model."

Danny realized he was taking IQ and Elys' time away from the celebration at home, and he said, "That's ok Son. Let's go home and celebrate your great news. I'm so happy for you."

IQ and Ely started up the trail walking hand in hand and talking excitedly. Stumpy and Sheba walked along with them and were still chuckling. Danny was the last one to leave and hesitated for about half a minute. The two dogs were still sitting side by side, and Danny decided to salute them. Sure enough, both dogs snapped off a sharp looking salute. Danny saw them as clear as day and quickly looked around for someone to confirm, but the others were now at least 50 yards ahead, and only Stumpy and Sheba were glancing back.

Stumpy and Sheba could barely walk straight because they were laughing so hard. They kept bumping into each other and Sheba said, "Oh, Stumpy, we are going to Level 3 if we keep this up, bwahaha!"

Stumpy said, "I haven't had this much fun for a long time. Did you see him salute across the wetlands? 'Achtung, Herr Wetlands!' Other walkers will think he lost his marbles, or at least has a big hole in the bag. I'm dying here, mwahaha."

IQ said, "What's gotten into these two? They look positively drunk."

Ely replied, "I'm just so glad that they get along so well. I love them both."

IQ suddenly remembered that he had his phone silenced and that he hadn't even told Harold and Olive the great news. He flipped it on and found multiple messages from Harold and Olive to call ASAP. He wondered if something was wrong at Microdots. He immediately called the office, and Harold answered on the first ring.

He said, "IQ, did you happen to take the 'Buzz' model off of my desk? It has something brand new on it worth tons of money. It's a prototype called 'Speck.'" He explained that the tiny dot on the rear of "Buzz" could be deposited like a fly speck and would record for about 15 minutes. It then could be picked up again by that same "Buzz." One "Buzz" could hold half a dozen "Specks" and could blanket a small room, then it could hide or leave the area until the opportunity arose to pick them up.

IQ said, "That's brilliant thinking, and yes, I picked it up. I apologize for not leaving a note or text. My dad swore that he saw something happen across the wetlands, and I attempted to use it to record, but I didn't get much on the front facing camera before I had to retrieve it. I have it safe and sound."

Harold said, "Put in this code on your phone and bring the video up again. The 'Speck' records constantly and then overwrites if necessary when still attached to 'Buzz.'"

IQ brought up the video and punched in the code. "Well, I'll be damned," he said. "It's as clear as day that they are saluting. Dad's not nuts after all."

By this time they were at IQ's drone, and Danny was far behind. They decided to show him the video at the house, since he had arrived at the trail by using his new squad car. They loaded the pets and called Harold to tell him that they were dropping off the new "Buzz." Ely called Maria and said they would be there in about 20 minutes. Then she called Olive and told her the great news. IQ could hear squealing noises of delight on the other end. The same thing happened when she called Faith. When IQ dropped off the new and improved "Buzz," he quickly congratulated Harold and Olive and told them they would be getting 5% shares of any money brought in from government sales of the new technology. He said they had to leave for the celebration party and would discuss everything the following day.

In the drone, Ely said, "I wish I had that outfit on that you like, but we have the pets who would be watching."

IQ suddenly got serious and replied, "Ely, do you think we would be disturbing or hurting the new twins by getting frisky? Can you ask your doctor? I don't want anything to happen to you or them! I love you too much to risk anything." He got kisses in return.

Finally, everybody had arrived at Danny and Marias' house, and everyone was talking at once about the wonderful ashes scattering service, Ely's pregnancy and the other cousins' engagements. Only Danny was acting strangely. He was holding Mei Lee in his arms and watching an approaching thunderstorm from the lanai. He was telling her about seeing the two dogs salute him and that nobody seemed to believe him.

Mei Lee said, "I believe you, Grandpa," and she gave him a kiss on the cheek. She could make anybody feel good, and he loved her as much as Maria did.

IQ said, "I have an announcement. Please, everybody, gather around the TV." IQ mirrored his phone to the massive 120" screen TV. There on the screen was a 15 second, crystal clear video of the two dogs sitting and saluting. "It appears that Dad was not crazy, or as Grandpa BD would say, 'His cheese didn't slide off his cracker.'"

Everybody was staring in amazement, and the video clip was replayed several times.

They were all saying, "There couldn't possibly be two more like Chewie, Braveheart, Stumpy and Sheba in the whole world, could there be?"

Bill was smiling and looking down from Level 2 at this wonderful family and thinking, "If they only knew, if they only knew!"

About the Author

Author Norman Merwarth, at age 80, is a firm believer in Toby Keith's song, "Don't Let the Old Man In." A Mechanical Engineering Graduate from Lafayette College, he is retired and lives with his awesome wife of 61 years, Carole, in The Villages, Florida. This book is a sequel to Bill's Lengthy Atonement, and he is already thinking of ideas for a third book. His wife likes to tease him about his grammar, and said, "You never met a comma you didn't like." Norman enjoys all sports, loves big dogs and walks around his favorite wetland's trail daily. He is a firm believer in Karma and you will see him greeting everyone with a smile and treating everyone according to The Golden Rule.